Protected by the Wolves

Lilly Wilder

Published by Lilly Wilder, 2023.

This is a work of fiction. Similarities to real people, places, or events are entirely coincidental.

PROTECTED BY THE WOLVES

First edition. January 1, 2023.

Copyright © 2023 Lilly Wilder.

ISBN: 979-8223724650

Written by Lilly Wilder.

Table of Contents

Protected by the Wolves

By: Lilly Wilder

Foreword

My life was at rock bottom. I'd always been afraid to live properly.

After a bad break up, my best friend Rachel convinced me to go to a bar called the Honey Pot and sing my heart out. She said that it wouldn't matter, that I'd never see anyone there again. It was true freedom. I could sing without consequences. It wasn't my usual place. It was filled with bikers. I was the odd one out.

But quickly things changed as I met Jack, Matt, and Buck. The three men who turned out to be more than men, wanted me in a way that nobody had ever wanted me before. My eyes were opened to a new world, a world of wolves...a world of desire. I was taken to their motorcycle club and they became my harem, my werewolves. I loved them and they protected me.

Protected by the Wolves

Chapter One

My hands trembled as I got up on the stage. The bar was sticky and a heavy smell hung in the air, a smell of liquor, beer and hard men. The crowd was raucous. A guitar screamed above them. My skin was warm and my heart fluttered. The whiskey made my mind hazy. It was supposed to quell my nerves, but it still felt as though a swarm of butterflies were flying around in my stomach. I gulped, but the lump in my throat wouldn't go away. I tried not to look at the crowd, but it was impossible. I wondered what they thought of me coming onto the stage, the blonde beauty. The bombshell. That's what Mom had always called me anyway; she'd always dressed me up as a little doll, making me into the image she wanted. She always called me beautiful, but I couldn't see it.

My friends had made me do this. The group of them were sitting at the table, a pitcher in between them all. They clapped and hollered loudly, but the noises got lost in the cacophony of the bar. All I wanted to do was turn and run outside, to feel the freedom of the night air and put this behind me. I wasn't ready. This wasn't right. I offered them a weak smile. Even I could feel it was false and I knew they must have felt it too.

The bar felt small and cramped. I could smell the sweat of the bikers and the rough men all around me. Their tattoos were illuminated in the dim light. The women who hung off their arms looked at me with scorn, wondering why a girl like me was in a place like this. I wondered the same thing. I hated my friends for making me do this, but deep down I knew it was something I needed to do. I had to crack the shell that was keeping me from enjoying the world. I had to break free, and the only way I knew how to do that was through song.

Everyone always told me I had the voice of an angel, a voice that could move the heavens and make grown men weep. There was something that happened when I sang. A spirit flowed through me and uplifted me. I was elevated to another plane and it was as though the world made sense. All the chaos and fear and doubt that usually plagued my mind was stripped away, leaving me with a pure feeling of belonging. When I sang I was at home. I was doing what I was meant to do, and I did it well. I felt free. Now was the time for me to share my gift. Rachel had persuaded me to do it.

"Think about it, Trish, you're never going to see anybody there ever again. Nobody is going to expect anything from you, so what's the harm? It's better to do it at the Honey Pot than anywhere else. You can be completely free of any fear because this is the only night you're ever going to go there," she'd said. It helped that the drinks were cheap, but it certainly wasn't the usual crowd.

As I walked onto the stage my gaze fell upon the crowd again and I noticed three men staring at me. I don't know what it was about them in particular, but when I noticed them it was as though a lightning bolt shot through me. Their faces were cast in shadow so I couldn't make out their features, except their eyes, which seemed to shine in an ethereal way.

The host welcomed me on stage. The open mic so far hadn't shown up any surprises. A few drunken people had warbled, but the crowd had been surprisingly supportive. It gave me confidence that it might be alright. The band was made up of long-haired rockers, grease monkeys from a bygone age where the music was raw and real, not over-produced and tuned to perfection.

I felt so small up there upon that stage and it brought back to mind the first time I had ever been on a stage. I looked to the side and was thankful not to see Mom there, pinning all her hopes on me. Back then I was young, naïve and scared. Mom wanted me to win competitions, to be a star. She said she always wanted to give me a better life than she had, but in truth I think that she just had a daughter so that she could have a second chance at life and try to make up for some of the mistakes she had made, not that she would ever admit that. No, any failure in life was a mixture of fate and bad circumstances, never a poor choice on her part. On that day I had stepped up to the microphone and nothing had come out when I opened my mouth. I ran off the stage, humbled and humiliated, and I swore that I would never do anything like that again.

But here I am. The host asked me my name. I answered him, but I was so nervous that I wasn't even aware of what I was saying. The lyrics were on a stand in front of me. I looked to them, hoping that I could try to forget about the crowd. I could already feel my chest tightening. Breath choked in my throat. I couldn't do this. Oh God, what the hell was I doing? I looked to the shadows on the side of the stage and felt the urge to run away and be swallowed by it all. Why did I let Rachel talk me into this? Why did I think doing this was a good idea? Better to just let the misery claim me than try to fight back against the onrushing tide.

But then the drummer smashed a note, the guitar screamed again, and the bar rumbled as the bass joined in. Suddenly I could hear my voice rising and expanding, filling the bar. I gripped the microphone stand for support so that I wouldn't melt into a puddle, but the emotions surged out of me. All at once I was vanquishing the trauma of my youth. All those times Mom had yelled at me and screamed at me to do better, all those times she had called me useless and worthless for not being able to do something as simple as sing.

I had never understood it. I never understood why she didn't seem to realize that I wasn't the daughter she wanted me to be. I never understood why she couldn't be like all the other Moms; why couldn't she hug me and wipe away my tears. Why couldn't she read with me instead of making me sing and perform different routines? At first it was fun, until I realized that the only reason she did it was to make sure I had it nailed down for performances.

That was the truth really. She thought life was only worth living if you had an audience. There was no point to anything else. It was all a show, everything designed to elicit an emotional response from the crowd. Unless people were gawking, gaping and applauding there was just no point to anything. What use was a life lived in the shadows? It was all made to be lived with a spotlight shining down on you, sparkling as the world watched on, a witness to talent and beauty, a witness to everything good in the world.

The only time I felt Mom was actually genuine was when she sang me to sleep. That was the only time I liked that she was different to other Moms. While they read their daughters to sleep, mine lulled me into slumber with sweet songs, and a voice that could break a heart. Mom had often told me that talent wasn't enough to make it, and she was proof of that. While she had a beautiful voice she never had the extra bit of luck that people needed to make it to the next level. That's why she tried to push me, tried to learn from her mistakes and make up for them through me. I suspected that if I had a little girl of my own Mom would have tried to make the dream come true through her as well, an endless parade of warriors ready to fight until finally one of us made it, as though it was only a matter of flinging enough of us at destiny until it finally buckled and gave Mom what she wanted.

But that wasn't to be.

The big C had gotten her before her time. Life hadn't really been kind to her, nor had I over the past few years. Once I got old enough to think for myself and fight back I was able to tell her how I felt and that I hated being on stage, that I never wanted to perform. When I told her that, you would have thought I'd threatened to kill myself. She was shocked and taken aback, as though I had stabbed her in the heart. She tried to make me feel guilty by telling me how much she had sacrificed to give me a chance, that so many other girls would have killed for a Mom like her. Maybe she was right, but I wasn't one of them.

Even up until the end Mom didn't understand the sacrifices I had made. I had basically lost my childhood to home rehearsals and nerves and anxiety. I was a wreck even just thinking about putting on a costume. Sometimes I still woke up in a cold sweat from nightmares about her driving me to an audition. I'd be crawling in the car, trying to escape the suffocating atmosphere, and before I went on I'd be having a panic attack. Mom used to just call it a part of the process and said that every great artist went through the same thing. It was an act of summoning something wonderful, she said, but I never understood why anyone should want to put themselves through that. It was sheer torture and it wasn't worth the pain.

I've never believed that things that are worth having are always difficult to get. I think things should be easy. I learned that not only from these panic attacks but also from Danny, my first love at school. Oh, how I was so enamored with him. Every time I thought of him my breath was taken away and I could barely think straight. My skin tingled and I was certain that the two of us were meant to be together. My feelings for him were so powerful; how could anything else happen? How could he not return the same feelings that I had? But I learned that just because you wanted something, even if you wanted it with all your heart and soul, you might not get it. Nobody deserves anything in this world. Mom had learned that through her efforts at trying to forge a career in show business. I had learned it at high school from the boy who broke my heart without even talking to me.

I shed a lot of tears over Danny. I've shed a lot of tears during my whole life, but none more so than when I learned Mom was dying.

It was bad enough learning she had cancer. She called me up after a long time of not speaking with her. I tried to harden my heart when it came to Mom because I knew that if I softened she would try and worm her way back in, and that would only mean trouble for me. I assumed she was calling for a favor, but then she blurted out that she had cancer. I immediately felt guilty for having spent as little time as possible with her over the past few years, and when I found out I raced to her and tried to take care of her as best I could. Having cancer didn't dispel all the trauma she had put me through and it didn't erase all the shouting matches we'd had over the years, but it does change your perspective on certain things. It certainly changed mine.

She told me that she only had a short time to live and she lamented all the things she had never done.

"But the one thing I'll never regret is having you. I know it wasn't easy, and I know your life hasn't always been what you wanted it to be...I know that I wasn't always what you wanted from a mother, but it's been a good life. I love you Trish, and I know that you can be anything you want. All I ever wanted was for you to be adored by the world," she had said.

"I was adored Mom, by you, and that's all I ever wanted," I said, tears streaming down my face. I pressed my head against hers as she took her last breath. I felt the rush of warmth against my skin and I sang her favorite song to her as she went to sleep for the last time. It was the same song I sang at the Honey Pot, a song for her. I knew all she wanted was to see me on stage so I made this one concession for her, a tribute to her memory, and hoped that she could see me from wherever she was.

I suppose a part of me hoped that it might bring her back in some way, that it might conjure some long-forgotten memory. I remembered all of the bad things of course, but they didn't seem so bad any longer. There was a void in my life. I had missed out on a lot of time with Mom because I held a grudge against her and it was startling knowing that I would never get that time back. All the emotion poured through me and seeped out into the bar, settling upon the crowd.

Mom had always told me that singing was the most intimate way to connect with the rest of the world, that when you showed your heart and put real, genuine emotion into the song everyone could latch onto it and take a part of it themselves, and the atmosphere in the room would rise and simmer and then erupt in an explosion of applause and adoration. I was always too stuck in my own mind to fully appreciate what she was trying to say, always too afraid of showing the innermost vulnerable parts of me, but now that I was on stage singing to this crowd of strangers I finally understood why she was so devoted to making it.

The feeling of being a part of something larger than myself was intoxicating. When I opened my eyes, even though my vision was blurred with tears, I could see them all watching me, hanging on my emotions. The song flowed from my heart and soul, radiant in its beauty and I was so attuned to them that the air almost seemed to glow. I stretched out my arms and felt as though I was floating. The music receded into the background and the song almost seemed to sing itself, as though it had taken complete control of me, possessed me. I like to think that it was my Mom's spirit claiming me and performing one last time, a spiritual duet between us that would lay to rest all the enmity and anguish I had felt over the years.

All eyes were rapt upon me. My skin tingled and my heart felt as though it was going to burst with pure emotion. The bar suddenly seemed more beautiful. Its scars faded and a resplendent aura emanated from the crowd. It was glorious. That was the power of a song. That was the power Mom was trying to teach me, and now I finally understood. After all this time, I finally understood.

The last note left my lips and the song faded. I bowed my head and wiped the tears from my eyes, gasping and panting for breath.

"Goodbye Mom," I whispered as I placed the microphone back. I bowed, thanked the band, and then left the stage to rapturous applause.

Chapter Two

As I walked back to my friends it felt as though there were wings on my feet. I was elated and exhilarated, my heart pounded and I struggled to catch my breath. My eyes glistened with tears and my clothes clung to my sweat-stained skin. I collapsed into the chair. Rachel leapt upon me and hugged me. The others there were more like acquaintances really, only Rachel truly mattered. She was the only one who knew the anguish I had been through.

"You've earned this," she said, and thrust a shot in front of me. I took it and felt the hot liquid burn my aching throat. I shook my head and felt a haze rise within my mind. The band was taking a break so the music had stopped for the moment. The bar was devoid of music, but the chatter of conversation gave it a pleasing ambience. My legs were like Jell-O and I was still trembling with raw emotion. Rachel handed me a proper drink after that, which I took gratefully, trying to gain at least a little hydration.

"You were amazing!"

"I had no idea you could sing like that!"

"How have you not done karaoke before?"

The people around me said all these things and more. I had never been very good with praise though. I dipped my head and my cheeks flushed. I mumbled something about not being very good and that this was just a special occasion, but I don't think they really understood. It did make me glow with pride. The praise and adulation of others was a powerful drug and I had to be careful to not enjoy it too much.

"This was just for my Mom," I said, and that was all I wanted to say on the matter.

"Are you sure about that?" Rachel asked. "You looked a natural fit up there. And you're better than anyone else that has sung tonight."

"Thank you," I replied, "but that doesn't mean anything. Performing could never bring me happiness. I've known that for a long time. Maybe if Mom hadn't pushed me so hard when I was younger..." I breathed, "no, it's not fair to put it all on her. I just don't think I'm the type of person who is comfortable with performing."

"You could have fooled me, and everyone else in this bar."

"That wasn't just me up there. Mom was with me in spirit," I said, smiling softly. "I could feel her presence."

"Okay," Rachel said.

"I know you don't believe me, and that's okay. But I did feel her. She was up there, singing with me. I know it won't make any sense to you, but it does to me. Things like this...there's more to the world than we understand. I know there's a little bit of magic and I know that she's still out there somewhere, at least her soul is, watching over me."

Rachel offered a pinched smile. I know she didn't believe me. Before all this I wouldn't have believed it myself. She probably just thought that it was wishful thinking on my part and that it was due to me not being able to let Mom go. Maybe that was part of the truth, but I could feel that there was more to the world than what we could taste, touch and smell. There had to be. Singing was a way to bridge the magical world with the physical one. It was spiritual and deep and meaningful, and it was also draining. I felt exhausted after having performed, but also glorious and delirious. I closed my eyes and I could see a vision of Mom forming in front of me, telling me that she was proud of me. I gazed towards the stage. I could feel the pull of it, but I steeled myself against the desire. It was just the rush of emotion controlling me, I thought, when the sensations faded and the cold light of day shone upon my face I would be back to sanity and back to my usual self, realizing that this life wasn't for me.

"I'm glad that you've made some peace with things," Rachel said, leaning over, resting a hand on my arm. It felt comforting to be in close contact with another human, with a good friend after all that I had lost. Rachel had been at the funeral with me. I had been pretty broken up and barely made it through the eulogy. A lot of tears had been shed and even when I was standing over the coffin I found it difficult to believe that she was really gone. I almost expected her to leap out and declare that it had all been a performance to garner some attention, but she hadn't. It almost seemed wrong that she wasn't alive to see the crowd that had gathered there, but in some ways I suppose that death was always the grandest performance that drew the grandest crowds. It was morbid, but I started to think what my own funeral would be like.

At my age, death always seemed like a vague, distant thing, elusive, lurking in the shadows. It was something that was easy to ignore and worry about in the far future. But then someone inevitably dies and it casts light on this darkest of things. Thinking about it is unavoidable. You question your life; everything in it and everything you have done. Suddenly none of it seems enough and there's a sense that time is running out. The world closes in and you know that, at some point, there's going to be nothing.

As exhilarating as my time on stage was, it was impossible to not be dragged down by my sadness. My head dropped and tears started to form in my eyes again.

"So now that you've done this, what's next for you?" Rachel asked. I didn't respond for a few moments.

"What do you mean?"

"Well, you said it yourself that you feel as though your life has been defined by your Mom. What are you going to do now that she's gone? Does performing up there change anything?" she asked.

In truth, I hadn't really thought about it. I hadn't thought about anything other than today. I just had to make it through today, but Rachel was right. Now that Mom was dead, now that the funeral was over I had to move on and find another path. I had always lived my life in Mom's shadow, even when we hadn't been speaking to each other. Everything I did had been to try and escape the parameters she had defined for me, although I couldn't say that I had done particularly well in that regard. When I spoke about her at the funeral it seemed as though she had done so much, and when I thought about what people would say in my eulogy I was left with a blank mind. In fact I didn't know who would give a eulogy.

"I don't think it does. I'm not going to copy Mom's life and try to be everything she wanted me to, now that she's gone. I wasn't lying when I said that this was a one time performance. I'm never going to sing in front of people again," I declared, probably a little too defensively.

"It's a shame because people really enjoyed it. But if you're not going to do that, then what are you going to do?"

"I have no idea." I'd never really given much thought to what I wanted to be, only what I didn't want to be. Mom had been so insistent on a single path that she had failed to teach me about all the other things I could do in life. She had been focused on one area, and so the world had seemed closed off and small to me. I had drifted for a while, working an ordinary job at an ordinary place, but I didn't want to do that forever. I had yet to discover my passion in life, and I was starting to wonder if I actually had one.

"Maybe I'll just continue as I am and see what happens for a little while," I said.

Rachel pouted and tilted her head towards me. "That's no way to live life. You can't just wait for things to happen. If you do that then you're never going to get anywhere, and you'll only grow bitter as you see everyone else making progress in life while you get left behind. There must be something you want more than anything else in the world. You can't just drift."

I wracked my brains to think, but there wasn't anything. The only thing I had ever shown any real aptitude for was singing, and that wasn't going to be an area I wanted to explore. I sighed and rubbed my temples. The band had returned and struck up a heavy, fast-paced tune that lured people onto the dance floor in front of the stage. The rest of our table went up. They tried to get me and Rachel to go, but

I shook my head and told them that I was still recovering from my performance. They shrugged and went off, blending into the crowd, leaving Rachel and I alone. We were so close I could smell the whiskey on her breath. Our words were clear through the blazing noise that rumbled through the rest of the bar.

"I know I can't, but I've never been someone who has had ambition. I've seen firsthand how much that can affect someone's life, and their relationships with others. I've conditioned myself to stop myself from thinking in that way."

"But there must have been something you've wanted," Rachel said. "Even if it's just a simple thing? Hell, I had a friend who all she wants out of life is to catch every Pokémon in every game. That's all she lives for, and when she does it she's happy enough and moves onto the next game. I wish we could all be satisfied so easily though..."

"You'll get to France one day. I want to walk through Paris and see your restaurant. You can make it."

"I'm not sure about that, not when I'm stuck working for Joe."

"You'll get there one day. It'll just take time. Maybe you should just up and leave, go to Paris in search of your dreams and never come back. It'd be like a movie!" I said.

Rachel chuckled and shook her head. "That only ever works in the movies. I don't speak a lick of French. If I went over there now I'd probably be laughed back to America, or I'd be stranded and I'd have to find some way to live on the streets. Besides, I could hardly leave you right now."

"Don't worry about me. I'll be fine, I always am," I offered a weak smile.

"You say that, but you don't even know what you want."

I looked around at the bar and saw all the people who appeared to be happy. Their moods were fierce and there was nobody drinking alone. I searched my mind, diving back into the furthest recess of my psyche to try and pluck an errant ambition from my muddled mind.

As my gaze drifted over the crowd, and a number of empty seats that had been vacated by people who had marched to the dance floor, I caught sight of the three men who had been looking at me on the stage. They were looking at me again, with such intensity in their eyes that I immediately looked away. My skin grew hot. Their eyes did not waver even though I had caught them. The thin hairs on the back of my neck rose and I turned back to Rachel, trying to put them out of my mind.

"There's only one thing I can think of, and you're not going to believe it," I said.

Rachel clasped her hands together and her eyes gleamed with excitement. "This sounds juicy!"

"It's really not. It's just that...growing up it was only ever Mom and I. I never knew my Dad and we didn't have any other family around, but there were so many times when I would have loved a big family. Don't get me wrong, Mom always tried her best to make things special and I was never left wanting on birthdays or at Christmas, but when I watched movies or read stories that had huge families spending time together I was always envious. I suppose it's that feeling of security you get from knowing there are a lot of people around you who are there to help you and support you no matter what. I've never had that and I've always wondered what it would be like. When I was younger I only ever had my Mom, and as much as she took care of me and worked hard to make sure that I had food on the table and clothes on my back, she was never the most empathetic person. When I went to her with a problem, sometimes I just wanted her to hug me and tell me that everything was alright, but she was always certain that it was my fault somehow. Like, you remember Danny?"

"Of course! How could I forget Danny?"

"Yeah, exactly, anyway, I told her that I liked him but he wasn't paying me any attention, and she kept saying that I was obviously doing something wrong. Either I wasn't wearing the right thing or I wasn't doing enough to get his attention. Not once did she tell me that maybe he just wasn't interested in me, and that was okay, that maybe I had an idea in my head of what things would be like with him, but that those thoughts didn't necessarily translate into reality. Somehow she had a way of making me feel like all the weight of the world was on my shoulders." I trailed off, growing despondent again. I hated to speak ill of the dead, but it was difficult when Mom had been such an overbearing presence in my life.

"Anyway, here's to Mom I guess," I raised my glass half-heartedly in a toast to her. I shot back the rough, dark liquid and swallowed it hard, forcing it down my throat, hoping that it would in some way take the pain away.

It might have dulled things for an instant, but the pain ran deeper than any alcohol could touch.

Rachel toasted along with me and offered me a reassuring smile.

"To your Mom. And to the future. If you want a family then you can go and find one for yourself. There's nothing stopping you. Look around; there are plenty of men in this bar and one of them might be the one you're looking for."

I cast my gaze around again, this time trying to purposefully avoid the three men who were dressed in leather and looking at me as though I was the only thing that existed. Had they been so moved by my performance that they were utterly transfixed by me, or was there something more? My stomach churned and fluttered and nerves tingled all over. I looked to other men. I couldn't say that any of them were my type because I didn't know what my type was. I suppose I always liked the idea of a strong man, someone who would stand up for me and protect me, someone who would be able to bear the weight of the world so that I could take a break for a little while. I wasn't sure that I was going to find it in this bar.

And those men...like a magnet my gaze was drawn back to them. Was it a trick of the mind? When I looked back another time they were facing each other, hunched in conversation. I strained my ears to try and overhear what they were saying. Mom had never told me that eavesdropping was bad. In fact she had only ever encouraged me to do it, because she said that we learned things from other people's conversation that we never would have learned otherwise. I trained my ears on the men, trying to fight through the blusters and bellows of the bar, but it was hopeless. My skin crawled. Were they talking about me? Was I just being egotistical?

I turned away. I could feel my skin growing clammy with sweat. My throat was dry despite everything I'd had to drink and the bar suddenly seemed cramped and confined. It was as though the ceiling was being lowered to just above my head, pressing down on me. All the people around me were hot and sweaty and the air was musky. My chest tightened as I was suddenly aware of them all swirling around me, like vultures buzzing, ready to feed on whatever carcass I left behind. Those dancing were a sea of people all caught in one undulating rhythm. The music surged through them, seizing them in their stupor, invisible strings that connected them like paper dolls. But I also knew that I was separate from them, a world apart, with my own sorrow and pain. The Honey Pot was a place for outsiders and in that sense I fit in, but as I looked around at all the people I only saw strangers. I didn't know how to connect with them, how to be one of them, and I was tired, so tired. All I could hear in Mom's voice was her saying 'go to them, go to them,' but my natural instinct was to fight it. Perhaps it would have been better if I had just gone and thrown myself into that sea of flesh and let the rhythm carry me away, but I railed against it, fought against my natural inclinations and I tore myself away.

"I need to get some air," I said, rising from the table before Rachel could offer to come with me. I pushed past the sweaty people, squeezing through their leather, trying to stop the music from pounding in my skull. It felt as though a drill was tearing my mind apart. With every step the door seemed to be farther away. I reached out, trying to physically pull myself forward out of the bar. Mean eyes looked at me, sneered at me. Hands clawed at me, trying to take advantage of what they saw as a weak woman. I wrenched myself away from their clutches, twisting away from this evil place, trying to escape the only thing that I could never escape; my own mind.

And then suddenly I burst out of the door, staggering out into the cool air. My feet crunched against the gravel and I almost fell, having to double over to catch my breath. I rested against the outer wall, feeling the entire bar rumble with the power of the music. The night was long and lonely. The moon hung like a silver coin in the sky, bright and wide, accompanied by the stars that were set like jewels against the murky, inky sky. The neon sign flickered above me, the honey pot looking as though it was going to pour its thick, sticky substance over my head. A row of bikes stood outside, and beyond that there were cars and trucks dotted all around the square parking lot. To my right there were a group of people huddled together, sharing hushed conversation and cigarettes. Wispy smoke rose in a cloud above them, the ends of the cigarettes burned amber. They paid no attention to me.

I walked along in the shadows, trying to hide from the world. Maybe that was the best place for me. I didn't know if I could ever find a family for myself. What kind of life could someone like me have? I had nothing to offer anyone. I had no idea how to even be a part of a family. I had failed as a daughter, and I felt as though I couldn't even mourn properly. All I wanted was to go home, crawl into bed, and curl up with some semblance of comfort to sleep the night away. I had done what I had come here to do. I had sang my heart out for Mom and I knew that she was pleased. Now I had to figure out how to do something for myself. I had to figure out how to live.

*

I was about to leave without telling Rachel. I knew it was bad of me, but I also knew that she'd understand. We had been friends long enough to allow certain misdemeanors to pass without comment. I just couldn't face going into that bar again, not with all those people and all that swirling music. Now that I was free in the fresh air I didn't want to return, I just wanted to escape. My skin prickled with goosebumps. I wore jeans, a casual top, and a denim jacket. It was hardly the most glamorous outfit, but it was comfortable and offered some protection against the elements.

Then I heard them. Their footsteps were heavy. Fear slithered down my spine even before I turned around to see them. The three figures were cast in shadow, looking huge and looming before my eyes. I gulped and hurried my pace. I didn't care if I was just being paranoid. Sometimes being paranoid saved lives. But my small strides were nothing compared to theirs, and they closed the distance between us without any trouble at all. Within moments they were upon me, their tall bodies blocking out the rest of the world. The light of the moon illuminated their faces and cast them in an ethereal glow.

One of them was taller than the others. His arms were crossed over his chest, and his biceps bulged. He wore a leather vest that left his arms exposed, and I saw a tattoo curling all down his right arm. His hair was pulled into a tight ponytail and he had a goatee. A single earring dangled from his ear. The man in the middle had his hands resting by his sides. He leaned slightly forward. His hair was lighter and wavier, looser. He was clean-shaven, and wore a heavy jacket. His lips were soft and sensual, his eyes were filled with mystery. The third was the shortest of the trio. His hair was the longest and he let it flow down past his shoulders. It was almost as long as mine. He had a long beard too, one that was braided, and he wore a peace symbol around his neck. His black shirt was open at the collar and the pendant nestled against a thick bed of chest hair.

"What do you want?" I asked in a trembling voice.

"We just want to know your name," the man in the middle said with a charming smile. "I'm Jack, this is Matt and Buck," he said, gesturing to his left and then his right respectively. Matt inclined his head and his long hair framed his face like a veil. Buck just nodded and grunted.

"I'm Trish," I stammered. I tried to keep my voice even, but it was difficult. My eyes darted around, looking for an escape route. I knew that I wouldn't have been able to flee into the night because they would have been able to outpace me, but if I could wriggle past them and make it back into the Honey Pot I could seek refuge with Rachel. There was safety in numbers, and I suddenly realized how much I hated being alone.

"We just wanted to thank you for the song you sang. It was amazing. Where did you learn to sing like that?" Jack asked.

"My Mom taught me," I replied. Maybe I was just being paranoid. They might have been fans after all. I shouldn't think the worst of people, but I couldn't ignore the alarm bells that were ringing in my mind. All I wanted was to get home.

"She must have been a hell of a woman," Jack said.

"Yes, she was. But look, I have to go. I was just heading home. It was nice to meet you and I'm glad you enjoyed the song. I'm sure there are going to be plenty of other people performing for the rest of the night. I doubt you'll want to miss any of those," I said, and tried to walk away, tried to peel myself away from the conversation. I wished that they would let me go and walk back into the bar. We lived in a world where men were supposed to respect women when they walked away politely, when they gave off signals that they weren't interested. I thought I was as plain as I could possibly be, short of saying that my Mom had died and I was grieving and I didn't want to be with anyone. I couldn't think of anything that would have been more of a buzz-kill than a dead parent, but at the time I wasn't thinking straight and I couldn't form coherent words. I stepped back, but they stepped forward, and I knew in that moment that I was in danger.

"None of them would sing like you. You're a real star," Jack said. My gaze shifted between the three men. Jack was doing all the talking, but the other two moved with him. It was as though they were all linked together. They moved as one, in complete harmony. I had never seen anything like it before and it was entirely unnerving. I tried to swallow my fear but it rose and swelled and grew. My lips parted as I stumbled back. I twisted my neck to look behind me.

"We don't want to hurt you. You don't have to be afraid. We just want to get to know you a little better," Jack said. There was something about his words. They seemed so slick and charming, so much so that I was almost enthralled by them, but one thing Mom had always taught me was to be careful, and to listen to my instincts whenever I felt afraid. My eyes were so wide with fear I thought they might pop out of my head. I managed to summon enough courage to cry out for help, but as soon as I did so Buck moved with surprising speed. He clamped a hand around my mouth. His skin was hot and leathery, and I struggled in his grip, but to no avail. His strength was bestial and I could no more escape his grip than I could escape being buried by six feet of snow.

His hand was upon my mouth and I could barely breathe. My eyes flared with panic as I tried to look beyond them, tried to catch the attention of the people who were smoking at the far end of the building, but my screams were muffled and my body hidden by these three men. My flailing arms were pinned to my side.

"Don't worry, it'll all be okay," Jack said. It was the last thing I heard before everything went black. His whisper echoed around my mind as Matt pulled out a small vial and wafted it in front of my nose. I breathed it in, struggling as I was for air. The smell was sweet and tempting and I felt a wave of serenity wash over me before I passed out, falling limp into Buck's arms.

Chapter Three

When I awoke for the first time I thought I was in a dream. The world rumbled beneath me and, as my vision became clear, I noticed that the world was a blur and upside down. My stomach lurched as panic gripped my heart and I remembered what had happened. I tried to scream, but my mouth was gagged and my hands were bound behind my back. My hair streamed out, whipping my face as the air made it dance. Roaring engines were loud in my head and drowned out my thoughts. The road was dark and empty. Exhaust fumes played havoc with my mind. I managed to twist around enough to see that I had been put in a side car. Jack was above me, leaning forward, his eyes on the road ahead. Matt and Buck flanked him. I pushed myself up and tried to catch the attention of anyone else on the road, aching to find some kind of salvation, but there was none to be found. The roads were dead. We were the only ones still alive and there was no hope for me.

I whimpered and by this point my movements were enough to catch the attention of Jack. He looked over at me and smirked. His eyes twinkled and for a moment I could have sworn that they turned golden. Then I fell unconscious again. Whatever concoction Matt had presented me with had played complete havoc with my mind. I couldn't think straight and I fell back into unconsciousness.

*

I stood on the stage again in the Honey Pot. This time there was no band behind me. I looked to the wings and my mother wasn't there either. I was on my own, by myself, feeling so small. I wrung my hands together in front of me and felt like a little girl going for an audition for a part that I knew I was never going to get. Those were the ones Mom always told me were the winners. People performed better when the pressure was on and you might as well shoot for the moon because you might catch a star or two on the way back down. But I always felt the pressure, and those were the worse auditions of them all.

I looked up to see who was going to be judging me and the breath caught in my throat as I saw it was them; the three men who held my life in their hands. Their gazes were inscrutable. In the dim distance there was the faint roar of motorcycle engines, and as I turned to look out of the windows of the bar I saw the outside scenery running by in a blur, as though the real world was bleeding into my dream.

Now was my opportunity to scream, I thought. Perhaps if I screamed in my dream, it might bleed back and I could free myself of my gag and escape. All it took was one person to hear me, to stop this terrible crime.

But when I opened my mouth fully and got ready to let fly the most desperate, soulful plea that has ever been heard, I was met only by silence.

"Sing for us," Jack said.

"You must sing," Matt added.

Buck grunted.

I tried to sing, I tried my hardest to make any sound come from my throat, but my voice had been stunned into silence. I gagged and choked and even reached into my mouth, as deep as I could, as though all I had to do was claw down, deep down into my soul, and pull out the words that had been lost inside. But there was nothing inside. The men frowned and looked disappointed with me. I could not speak. I could not scream. I could do nothing but stand there and feel like a failure.

I looked around desperately for Rachel, but she was nowhere to be seen. There were only the men there. I hoped that I might at least be reunited with the spirit of my mother, but the area was devoid of any other presence. I was alone, truly and utterly, and I didn't know how I was going to cope. I looked to the men and waited for them to tell me any kind of reason why they had brought me here, why they wanted me to perform for them, but they just sat in silence and said nothing. Tears streamed down my face. I looked down at my feet and noticed that my ankles were shackled to the stage, as though I was destined to stay there for the rest of my life, unable to move until I sang, but the song had been lost in the caverns of my soul. I tore my blurred gaze away from them and faced the wide window.

Outside in the blurred world that rushed by so quickly, so quickly it appeared as though I was being left behind, there was but one thing that was constant; the silver moon. It throbbed and pulsed, and seemed to expand in my mind. Its silver light was blinding and it filled my vision. I had to blink, but even then the flash overwhelmed everything. It filled the bar and the men disappeared into the bright brilliance. I winced and begged for mercy, but then the light engulfed me and I wasn't sure I would ever be the same again.

*

A fragrant scent drifted through my mind and my eyes fluttered open. I felt groggy and my hands immediately fell to my aching stomach. I coughed and spluttered, feeling as though I wanted to throw up the contents of my stomach, but nothing came out. I gasped for breath as I brushed the hair away from my face.

"Drink this," Matt said. As soon as I was made aware of their presence I scrambled back, getting as far away from them as I could. I hit a wall and clung to it for dear life. My eyes were still wide with panic and I could barely speak. I shook my head and tore at my hair.

"Please," he continued, "this will make you feel better. I promise."

His tone was kind, as were his eyes when I dared to look at them, but how could I believe him? He had tricked me and my senses somehow, stolen my consciousness and goodness knows what they had done to my body. I patted myself down and almost groaned with relief when I realized that my clothes were still intact and that nothing felt different about my body, but I knew that could all change within an instant if I wasn't careful. My guard was still up and I pressed my lips together tightly, shaking my head, letting Matt know that I wasn't going to take anything he gave me, willingly.

"How long is she going to be like this?" Jack asked.

"Unless she drinks this it's going to take a while for her system to work through the other drug. I did tell you it was risky," Matt said.

"It was a risk we needed to take. And it was safer than Buck whacking her over the head." Jack frowned and his eyes bore into me with white hot intensity. I wasn't sure that I had ever been scared of anyone as much as I was scared of him in that moment.

"What do you want with me?" I asked in a trembling whisper. My voice was so quiet it was barely audible.

"You'll find out soon enough. The sooner you drink that, the better. I'll tell you everything when you have your mind back, but don't worry. You're safe with us," he said.

"I don't believe you," I replied.

Jack didn't say anything to that.

"Leave the drink with her. She'll come to her senses soon," Jack said. Matt seemed uncertain, but he followed Jack's orders and left the plastic cup by the door. Buck's absence was noticeable.

"Do you really think she's..." Matt said as they left the room, but they closed the door, cutting off the sentence before I could hear what they were going to say. I groaned as I fell against the wall. My body was rigid with tension and I was exhausted as so many thoughts whirled around my mind. I breathed deeply and tried to remember all the lessons I had learned. Mom had taught me from a young age that the world was not kind to women. Predators were everywhere, always trying to take what they wanted even when you didn't want to give it to them, but this...I never thought I would have been in this situation.

No.

I had to think.

They hadn't done anything to my body yet. I still had time. There was a way to escape. There was always a way to escape. My mind was still haunted by the dream. The blinding moonlight was still there when I blinked and I was so afraid that when I opened my mouth no words would come out. My throat was raw and scratchy, as though I had swallowed glass. My muscles ached. I had no idea how long I had been unconscious or where we were. We could have been travelling all night as far as I knew, and that meant we could have gone over state lines. I thought of Rachel and wondered if she had realized yet that I had gone missing. I cursed myself for leaving the bar so hurriedly. She would have probably assumed that I had gone home and wouldn't bother checking on me until the morning, and I was notoriously bad at shutting myself away, so she might not realize that I had gone missing at all for days.

I was paying the price for my isolationist tendencies. I didn't even have my cell with me as I hadn't bothered to take it to the bar. I'd wanted a night away from people bothering me.

I had no way to contact the outside world. I was completely alone, at the mercy of these three men, and I had no idea what they wanted.

I breathed deeply and tried to compose myself. The first thing Mom taught me was that I had to remain composed no matter what. If I panicked then they were winning. I had to ensure that I was of a clear mind so that I could get out of this situation. I closed my eyes and practiced the breathing techniques that Mom had taught me. They had never worked to calm me down before a performance, but this time they did. I counted to nine as I inhaled and exhaled, filling my lungs with air, and gradually my heart rate slowed and I was able to have a better grip of the situation.

After this, I took the opportunity to take measure of my surroundings. The room was dark. There was a small, narrow window high on the ceiling, which was about ten feet high, and the walls were sheer, so there was no hope of me climbing up to at least get a glimpse of my surroundings. There was a single bed in the other corner of the room. I pulled myself over to it. The blanket was scratchy and the mattress creaked as I placed my weight on it. I looked to the window and gripped the cast iron bed frame, groaning as I tried to pull it towards the window, but it was far too heavy for me to do anything with it. I put all my strength into it, but it barely budged.

The floor was stone and the room was devoid of anything else, aside from the cup of drink that Matt had left. I gazed at it cautiously, warily, and eventually made my way over to it. My throat gasped for some kind of relief. I whimpered and sobbed, despite my best efforts to not show any weakness but there was only so much resolve a girl could muster. I licked my lips as I got closer to it and wrapped my hand around the mug. The liquid was gold in color and it smelled sweet. As soon as I brought it to my lips I was filled with the irresistible urge to taste it, even though I was afraid that it was another kind of drug that would render me unconscious.

But they already had me imprisoned. There was no need for them to drug me again, especially not like this. They had me and they could easily overpower me. I know that when things seemed too good to be true they usually were, but in this instance I was inclined to at least take a chance on trusting the drink. After all, what else could happen to me? What could possibly be worse than my current situation?

I tilted the mug towards me and the thick liquid, which had the consistency of a smoothie and the taste of honey mixed with fruit, slipped between my lips and settled over my tongue. I gulped down one mouthful and then, when I didn't immediately vomit, I finished off the rest of it greedily, wiping away the trickling remnants that lingered around my mouth. In fact I was so thirsty that I ran my finger inside the mug to get the last drops, and then sucked them off, surrendering to the relief that ran through my body.

I placed the cup back by the door and retreated to the bed. I sat with my legs pulled into my chest and watched the door like a hawk, waiting for any of them to come in. I thought about my next move. I could either try to fight them and make life so difficult for them that I was more trouble than it was worth to them. That was a solid plan, but it also led to the possibility of getting very, very hurt, and possibly killed. The other way was to act as though I had been defeated, to follow whatever orders they had for me and to surrender completely until I found a way to break free and survive, if such an opportunity presented itself.

As I thought about these possibilities I realized that in some ways I had been training for this all my life. Mom had always wanted me to put on a captivating performance and now I was going to have to do exactly that for the benefit of my captors. But first I needed to understand what they wanted from me, and why they had kidnapped me.

Chapter Four

"I'm ready to talk!" I yelled, as I beat my fists against the door. I shook my hands as pain throbbed. I'd been at it for a while now, and nothing had happened. I kicked and screamed, and then, eventually, gave up, frustrated. I sank on the floor, resting against the bed. I dared not lie down even though the lumpy comfort of the mattress was enticing, afraid that if I lay my head down I would fall asleep and be at their mercy, even more than I already was. My hands clawed at my hair. I dragged my eyes down, but thankfully my throat felt a lot better. Whatever had been in that strange liquid had been a healing elixir and I didn't feel any ill effects, although part of me was waiting for the other shoe to drop and all the pain in the world to flood through my body.

For the time being though, it seemed as though these strange men were keeping their word. I wasn't feeling the effects of a hangover either, which was strange. My head throbbed, but it was more from tiredness than anything else. It had been a whirlwind of a day and the Honey Pot seemed to be so far away. Would I ever see it again? Would I ever see the light of day? It was so cruel to leave me waiting here, festering, with the torment of my own mind, trying to figure out their intentions. Aside from the obvious I had no idea what they wanted from me. I'd heard lots of horror stories about human trafficking. I was probably the kind of girl they liked to prey on the most; I had no family, no ties. Barely anyone would miss me. I would just be one of those forgotten, missing people, the kind you hear about all the time. People look into it, they're captivated by the mystery for a little while but eventually they lose interest because their own life takes over. It's always the same way, and in the end these people just become a name lost in the ether. The essence of the life is lost, the very meaning is taken away.

I ran through old show tunes in my mind to try and stop myself from going crazy. I had no way to tell the time, as it seemed perennially dark through the window. All I could do was wait for one of them to come and see me. My destiny was in their hands.

*

I could feel myself falling asleep. My head drooped as though it was pulled by invisible weights. The bed, as lumpy and uncomfortable as it was, seemed inviting. I was beginning to get hungry and thirsty again. I walked around the room in an effort to keep my muscles moving and the blood flowing, although the room seemed to get smaller all the time. I picked up the blanket and placed it on the floor, and then I lay with my back flat against the surface. I stretched my lithe body and tried to still my mind, using the calming techniques of yoga to steady my rampant nerves. It was easy to relax in a calming environment with scented candles and meditative music playing in the background, far harder in a dark room where danger lurked behind the door.

Then, it opened. Jack was standing there. Matt was behind him.

"Ah, good, she's had the drink," he muttered, then he turned to me directly. "How are you feeling?" He spoke a little more loudly than usual, in the same manner as one would talk to an older relative who was hard of hearing.

"Don't worry Matt, I'll take care of this," Jack said, before I could reply. Jack stepped into the room and leaned down, picking up the cup, and then handing it to Matt. Matt seemed perturbed, but he didn't vocalize his dissatisfaction.

"Are you sure you want to be left alone?" Matt asked. Jack smirked and turned to the other man.

"Don't worry, you'll get your chance to be alone with her."

Something about the way he said it made my skin crawl. I sat bolt upright and pulled the hair away from my face, trying to show even a hint of defiance. Matt closed the door and I was left alone with Jack.

He wore a leather jacket that hung slack over his shoulders. His body was slight, but he still had a good build, he had just looked more slender when compared to the bulky form of Buck. Jack pursed his lips and took a few steps into the room, but he maintained some distance from me. He studied me carefully, resting his chin against his hand. His boots were heavy, and they thudded whenever he walked. His gaze was piercing and I summoned the courage to lift my gaze to meet his. I remembered the brief flash of gold that had greeted me when I had awakened midway through the ride, but there was no trace of gold in his eyes now and I decided it must have been a trick of the mind.

The air around me simmered with tension and I vowed that I wasn't going to speak first, but Jack waited and waited, he stared and stared, and eventually the pressure made me crack. The palpable tension was unbearable.

"What do you want with me?" I asked, hoping that this time he would offer me an answer. My head dropped as I asked the question and the words fell out of my mouth without much force. I put on the air of a defeated woman. It wasn't too far from the truth. I only lifted my eyes to see if there was some hint of an expression flickering over his face, but there was nothing I could glean from him.

"Everything will become clear in time. But first I want to make sure that you're okay. Are you feeling well?" he asked.

"About as well as I can be considering the circumstances. Why won't you tell me what you want with me? You can't just bring me here without permission. Why have you kidnapped me?!" I asked, the words coming out in a flurry. Jack studied me for a few moments more. I had no idea why he was being this mysterious. Fear mixed with anger and I felt just as I had done in all those auditions in my youth; as though my destiny lay in the hands of other people. I had always hated that feeling, the feeling of powerlessness. It was perhaps the worst feeling in the world. I had always wanted my life to be my own, to be the arbiter of my own destiny.

I realized then that it could never be the case. First it was my mother, now it was these men. But then again, could I really blame them? What had I done with my life that was so great? At least they had a plan for me, or so I assumed. Mom certainly did. I had no idea. I was just drifting along. Maybe they could sense this. Maybe that's why they took me. I'd seen a few true crime things; people always said that kidnappers chose their victims carefully. I had nobody who was particularly going to miss me. I didn't have a big impact on the world. I was practically nothing, an empty shell. I swallowed my fear. It didn't take much of an appearance to seem demure and submissive. I bowed my head, allowing my hair to fall around me like a veil. My hands trembled.

"Come for a walk with me," he said. His voice was soft, but there was something in the way he said it that suggested I didn't have a choice. No matter how gentle they might have seemed or how much they said they were going to take care of me, I had to remember that I was their prisoner, and like any good prisoner I was going to try to escape.

*

I followed him out of the door. I was quite frankly surprised that he didn't put a leash on me, or at least some handcuffs. He must have been that confident that he could handle me if I tried to escape. Well, I wasn't going to try to escape just yet. That was perhaps the worst thing I could have done. I needed to get them comfortable, to lull them into a false sense of security. Only then could I hope to escape. I had to keep my wits about me, and observe as much as I could. Unfortunately, it didn't help that the place was dark. Jack led me down a dark corridor. I could hear sounds coming from other parts of the building; murmurs of conversation and some music playing. There was also the roar of a motorcycle as well, fading as the rider drove off into the distance.

Another door opened, this one to the outside world. The night was dappled with moonlight. The air was fresh and cool. It couldn't have been too long until dawn rose. The fading night was beautiful and ethereal. Shadows danced and the leaves of trees fluttered as the night breeze wafted by. Owls hooted and deep in the distance a wolf howled. Jack's ears pricked up and his gaze drifted towards the origin of the noise. I didn't pick up on the significance of that at the time.

The grass was covered in dew. The forest was a place of mystery, stretching out for miles all around. It was an easy place to lose oneself in, and I was starting to get an idea of how I might escape. I turned around to see the back of the building. It was low and wide, with a slanted roof. A long road stretched out in front of it, leading to eternity on either side. There were no twinkling lights of a city; a sight that I had grown used to. Out here it felt as though we were the only people in the world, in the only place that existed. It was easy to feel lost.

We walked about halfway between the building and the edge of the forest. Fear clutched my heart as it felt as though we were marching towards my doom, but then Jack stopped abruptly and lifted his head to the moon with a reverent gaze, in silent worship. I wasn't sure how I should act or what I should say, so I remained quiet until he spoke.

"She's beautiful, isn't she?" he eventually said. He closed his eyes and smiled.

"Yes, she is." I couldn't deny that the moon looked even more impressive than usual, as did the stars. I was used to living in the city, so they were always hidden behind the bright neon lights that twinkled in a city that never really slept. The moon was just a part of the scenery, a pale dot in the background, receding behind the flashing lights, promising fame and fortune, capturing attention away from what was truly beautiful in the world. But out here the moon and the stars had no equal. They glittered with resplendent beauty against the inky backdrop of the night sky and it was easy to believe that miracles could happen.

"I was told a story when I was a child, that the moon was once a woman who wanted to be near the sun. One day she leapt up from her home, leaving her village and her family behind, and she became the moon, for of course the sun was too warm to get close to. I used to try it myself. One day I jumped from the top of my home. I broke my leg," he laughed dryly. "My mother scolded me and told me to never listen to stories again, but ever since that day I've wondered if there's a way to touch the moon."

"That's a lovely story," I lied. I didn't particularly care about his childhood, his mother, or the goddamned moon. It had become quite clear to me that he wasn't going to listen to my demands, so there was no use in begging him to tell me what he wanted with me. He would tell me in his own time, or not at all, and I just had to live with that. But I was already tracing a path with my eyes, looking to the forest and thinking about where it might lead. As I peered into the darkness I was thankful for the brightness of the moon as it highlighted certain landmarks, like a mountain to the right of me. The jagged peak cut out some of the stars and I thought that would make a good direction for my escape. I could almost see myself running through the forest, losing myself in the darkness as I escaped this most dangerous situation. There was an urge in my heart to do so then, but my feet were rooted to the spot. My skin crawled as I thought of the way Jack's hands would pull me back and throw me to the ground, how even though the grass was soft and wet it might as well have been daggers stabbing into me.

"After that Mom told me that the only way to touch the moon was through a song. Do you believe in magic Trish?" he asked.

"Magic? I...I can't say that I do."

"Really? You should...you conjured magic over the entire bar with your song. Magic doesn't have to be from witches and wizards and all those sorts of things. It's deeper than that, more personal. It happens when you expose your soul to others. They see something pure, something vibrant and alive, and they respond to that. When you sang every single person in that bar was transfixed by you, spellbound. Hearing you sing was as beautiful as seeing the moon like this."

His words were beautiful, and if he had spoken like this at the bar I may well have gone home with him and given him whatever he wanted, but he had already taken me away by force, ripped me from the night without mercy. I wasn't going to let him get away with doing everything he wanted. When I replied there was cold steel in my voice.

"That might well be true, but that doesn't help me at the moment. What is this place? What do you want with me?" I asked again, tiring of his musings on magic and the moon. It seemed crazy, and the more he spoke the more I wondered if this was some kind of dangerous cult. There were moments when he didn't seem to be making any sense. It was as though he saw the world in a different way than anyone else and I wasn't entirely sure how to handle it. I glanced down to make sure that he wasn't holding a knife or other weapon in his hands. I was afraid that I might be a sacrifice to the moon.

He turned his head. There was a strange look in his eyes, and once again I was reminded of that moment when I had seen gold in them. Was that just a trick of the mind or was there something more? I was so tired and my mind was strung out. It was easy for me to believe in the dangers of the world. In a place like this the impossible seemed more believable and things like magic rose from the ground, seeping into every pore, until daylight would come again and wash it away in its brilliant light.

"I want you for your song Trish, for your song and for everything that means," he said.

I frowned. That still didn't make any sense. He turned away from me and it seemed to be the only answer he was going to give.

"And what is this place?"

"We're a motorcycle club. We're small, but it means a lot to us."

"A motorcycle club?" I asked skeptically, folding my arms across my chest. Jack wasn't what I expected. He seemed aloof, almost as though he wasn't really there. "And do you make a habit of kidnapping innocent young women?"

"No, we don't. Just you," he said.

His words took me by surprise. My breath caught in my throat and I wasn't quite sure what to say about that. I didn't think there was anything special about me. My hackles rose and my skin prickled with unease. I shifted my weight between my feet and furrowed my brow even deeper, wanting to snap at him, wanting to lash out in anger. He was so sure of himself, so confident that I wouldn't dare do anything against him, that he wasn't even worried that I might escape. And what was so special about me anyway; that I was vulnerable? That I had no family? That I was practically alone in this world without any direction or purpose? Those things didn't make me special...they made me a failure.

"And what if I just ran away right now? What if I fled into the darkness and disappeared into the forest? You might think you're stronger and faster than me, but you have no idea. You don't have your bike here and you don't have your cronies. Maybe I could have a chance," I dared to express the idea of a challenge and instantly his hand shot out to grip my arm, so tight that it left bruises. His eyes flashed with anger.

"Try it," he growled. There was such animal intensity in his voice that I could barely think straight. All thoughts of challenging him disappeared from my mind as I knew he wasn't going to let me go. I pulled my arm away.

"Get your hands off me!" I cried. I stepped away a few paces, retreating back to the building we had just left. I nursed my arm. Pain throbbed and a hopeless feeling entered my heart. I knew this wasn't going to be easy, but I dreaded what they might do to me.

Jack turned back to the moon.

"Your place is here with us now. It has been decided. Go and rest. You shall learn more tomorrow."

"Decided? By who? By what? I haven't decided!"

"Go and rest," he said again, a growling undercurrent in his voice once again. I stared at him, wondering for a moment what would happen if I did lash out at him and claw at his eyes, if I slashed with my nails and tried to run away. The air was open and the night was all mine, but fear cowed me and gripped me completely. My hand trembled. It was as though an invisible force put pressure on my hand and would not allow me to lift it up. I was trapped completely, unable to strike out at him, or at my freedom.

I felt like a failure, just as I had done so many times at the auditions. I slunk away back to my prison, back to the only building in sight. Jack spoke with such certainty and threat. I knew that, somehow, even if I tried to escape he would hunt me down and find me. Even if I made it into the depths of the forest or to the summit of the mountain, he would be there, knowing my every move before I made it. A small sob erupted in my throat as I returned to my prison. My shoulders slumped. I had the air of a defeated woman. I was still so tired. I had never thought of myself as one to surrender so easily, but it was a habit that I had adopted in life. It had taken everything I had to break free of Mom's control and that was a process that had taken years.

It wasn't so easy to escape as you might think. I had no idea where to go or even in which part of the country I was in. I wanted to flee, but there was something inside holding me back, and every time I did I saw Jack's eyes flashing inside my mind. In the depths of his gaze I saw the control he had over me, the utter certainty that I would never do anything to disobey him and it was so overwhelming I found it impossible to resist.

Perhaps there was magic in the world after all. Perhaps he had cast a spell on me. They had given me an elixir that had cleared my mind, but what else had it done? The world was a dark place and I was but a single soul, adrift and alone with nobody to turn to. I certainly wasn't going to get any sympathy from Jack. I turned to the stars before I went back into the building and wished that Mom was still around. Say what you like about her, but she was fierce and she wouldn't have allowed anyone to treat me this way.

I took a final look at Jack before I went inside. He was standing there, as still as a statue, staring up at the moon as though it was a goddess. It was a foolish story, I thought, and I didn't much care for what he said about singing. My voice wasn't anything special. He had some idea that I was special, that I was more than I actually was. How could he know these things when I didn't even know them myself?

I shook my head as I returned inside. I felt certain that they must have taken the wrong person. If they were looking for someone special then they hadn't chosen well in me. Perhaps I'd get lucky and they'd realize their mistake before too long and return me to the sorry excuse I had for a life.

I sometimes wondered what would have happened had I continued on the path Mom wanted for me. If I had managed to overcome my anxiety, and not let myself get so bothered by the pain of performing or the expectations and demands of the lifestyle, could I have actually made it? I doubt I would have become anyone famous, but I might have carved out a niche for myself, a comfortable life where I didn't have to worry about anything. It was easy to think about a better life after I had been kidnapped though. In fact I'm not sure that the magnitude of what had happened had sunk in yet. All I could think about was a parallel version of my life, one that was better in every respect. To be honest it didn't take much imagination, considering that it couldn't get much worse. All the decisions I had made had led me to this point, and I dreaded to think what the decisions I would make in the future would lead me to. I had my hand on the door to the building. I closed my eyes. A tear squeezed through my eyelids and trickled out. I could have walked away, maybe I should have, but I was filled with fear that it could mean my death. The way that Jack had hissed at me...I couldn't deny his power. They had already succeeded in kidnapping me once and I had no doubt they would find me again.

He was so confident, that he was willing to let me walk away by myself without an escort. I got the sense that he wasn't the type to misplace his confidence. I still wanted to escape but I would have to wait and bide my time. I couldn't risk angering them when there was still so much that was uncertain. I had escaped their wrath so far, but I couldn't be sure they wouldn't kill me.

I clutched my arm again. In the faint moonlight I could already see the bruises start to bloom upon my skin. Jack had marked me, and the thought of it made me tremble.

Chapter Five

I felt at my lowest ebb as I returned to my cell. My head hung and my feet dragged across the floor. I wished that I could have been braver and stronger. I wished that I could have had the strength to fight, but my mind had cracked and every time I thought of resisting, I was filled with fear. I just couldn't bring myself to do anything like that when there was so much against me. It felt as though the world had caved in on me and there was no hope of escape.

But as I walked, I passed a door, and behind it I heard murmuring conversation and soft music. There was a clink of glasses and some people were louder than others. Without Jack accompanying me I was free to linger and press my ear against the door to try and glean whatever information I could.

"Do you think she's the one we've been waiting for?"

"I hope so, we've been waiting for long enough."

"We'd better make sure to keep her hidden. We can't let the Hunters get wind of this."

"We won't. The Hunters are just arrogant upstarts who think they know more than they really do. We've dealt with their kind before and if they try anything we'll slap them down into place."

"I still think we should have asked her. This kidnapping business doesn't sit right with me."

"What would you have done? Told her the truth?" There was a lot of laughter at this comment. "Good luck with that. This is the best way. Jack knows what he's doing, and you care too much. We need her and that's the end of it."

It felt as though there was going to be more to the conversation, but at that point footsteps came near the door and I got scared. I squealed a little as I didn't want to be caught eavesdropping and find out what punishment would wait for me. I skipped back into my small room and closed the door, and then I retreated to the bed.

Even though I couldn't hear properly, I was certain that two of the voices I heard were Buck and Matt's. There were a couple of others I didn't recognize, and it was unclear exactly how many members the motorcycle club had, but at least there was one person who wasn't in favor of the way they had treated me, and I hoped that it would provide a window that I could take advantage of. But the way they spoke of needing me...it just didn't make any sense. What kind of thing would they need me for? I didn't understand...I needed answers. I needed to know what was going on and why they thought I was so important.

And what were these Hunters? Perhaps they could provide my salvation if they were the enemy of Jack's group. My mind whirled as I clutched the flat pillow and sobbed myself to sleep. It was soon wet with my tears and I wished that I was anywhere else. At least when I slept I could be free of the horror that pervaded my mind, although I was terrified of my dreams too.

*

I awoke feeling lethargic and aching. I checked myself as the daylight streamed through the narrow window. It was so bright that it illuminated every corner of the room, and highlighted how dreary everything was. A copper pipe reached down in the corner and led all around to a metal radiation. The bed frame was cold and sturdy, and the blanket was scratchy and stained. I preferred it when it was shrouded in darkness. I wiped my eyes and caught sight of the bruises on my arm. I hadn't realized Jack had gripped me with such strength. I gently brushed my skin and winced. There were three round bruises, and I wondered how many more there would be by the end of this.

I rubbed my face and swallowed. My throat was dry and my stomach rumbled. I hoped that someone would be along with some breakfast soon. Now that I could see better, I tried to clamber up the pipe and reach the narrow window. I thought that if I could reach it I might at least be able to squeeze something through, but it was to no avail. It remained tantalizingly out of reach. I could feel some of the warmth of the air outside and I could see the blue sky, but it might as well have been an alien world.

Eventually the door opened and Matt was there. He brushed his long hair away and his clothes hung off him like a cloak. He glanced towards me and there was kindness in his eyes, and a hint of regret. I was certain that it had been he who expressed reservations during the conversation I had eavesdropped upon and I was keen to exert some influence to exploit this.

He set down a tray that had upon it a glass of juice and a bacon sandwich. It wasn't my usual breakfast of choice; I much preferred something more nutritious and healthier, but clearly I didn't have a choice. He went to leave, but I couldn't let him. Not yet.

"Wait...Matt...isn't it?" I asked. Matt paused. He stood halfway in the room and had his hand on the door handle, ready to close it at a moment's notice.

"Do you think I could eat this somewhere else? This room it's...it's not very nice and I just feel so dirty," I winced and rubbed my arms, casting my gaze away from him, to appear even more vulnerable than I felt. My request lingered, and the more time he stayed the more chance I thought there was of him granting my request.

Eventually he sighed. "I can take you somewhere else, but we can't stay for long," he said, and held the door open. I picked up the tray and followed him out into the hallway. The juice sloshed inside the glass. We passed the door I had eavesdropped behind and then went into one beyond that. It was a small room, a lounge area with a couch, TV, table and chairs around it. There were cards strewn about the table and empty nut shells that had been cracked. The room had the stale smell of beer, peanuts and grease, as though these smells had been imbued into the walls and the ceiling. A triangular banner hung on the wall, pointing at an angle. One word was depicted on it; 'Howlers'.

"Is that the name of your club?" I asked as I took a seat on the couch. I turned my nose up at the stains and the torn leather, but I had sat on worse. Matt placed the tray beside me. I took the food and tried not to wolf it down. I didn't want to betray my desperation. The bacon was crispy and the bread was soft. It was a good sandwich and I immediately felt better, but I was still on my guard.

"Yeah, it is," Matt said, looking up with reverence at the wall. There were other pictures hanging on the wall, and as I looked more closely I saw that they depicted the club through different eras. When it began in a bleached photo from another era there were dozens of them, and over time that had dwindled down to today, where there was just a handful. "There used to be so many of us," he said.

"What happened?"

Matt's head dropped and he pursed his lips. "It's just the way of life. A lot of people don't have much time for it anymore. Sometimes I think we're a relic of a bygone age but, hopefully our time will come again."

"I'm sure it will, I mean, who wouldn't want to be a part of a group that kidnaps innocent people?" I snapped, and then swallowed a mouthful of juice. Unlike Jack, I didn't get the sense that Matt was as confident or as domineering, but I wanted to test it. By his reaction, I knew that I was right.

"I'm sorry about all that," he mumbled, averting his gaze because he couldn't dare look at me. The corners of my lips twitched. It seemed as though I had found the weak link, although I was still on my guard and wasn't going to get ahead of myself. But I hoped that he at least might give me some answers.

"Are you? Really? My mother always said that if you were truly sorry about something then you wouldn't have done it in the first place."

"I am," Matt said, "but I didn't have a choice."

I let out a dry laugh. "That's the excuse you're going to use? Okay...I can see the type of people I'm dealing with here. Of course you had no choice other than to kidnap me. I guess I'm just the most important woman in the world," I threw up my hands in frustration and rolled my eyes. It worried me that Matt didn't say anything. He had a strange expression on his face and seemed afraid to look at me, and yet he couldn't stop. Whenever I lifted my gaze he always averted his. There was something sweet about it, really. I finished the sandwich and wiped the crumbs away from my mouth. I felt the tang of cold juice as I finished up the drink and set them on the couch beside me. I pushed myself up from the couch and dipped my head, swaying my hips in a way that always got the attention of men. I played with the ends of my hair, twirling it around my fingers and walked up to him.

When he noticed, he stepped back, until he was pressed against the wall. He smelled of the earth and of the forest. I looked up at him with alluring eyes. I wasn't at my best, but given the surroundings and the way he looked at me I doubted very much if he had many women acting this way around him.

There were barely inches between us as I lifted my bright eyes and pressed my hand against his chest.

"Is that true Matt? Am I the most important woman in the world?" I asked softly, the words dripping off my tongue like honey. I could feel Matt's body grow rigid with tension and his heart quickened. His breath came out in short bursts and still he could not look at me directly, as though I was the sun and he avoided looking at me for his own safety.

"No...this...it isn't time," he muttered, and then pushed me away. He ran his hand through his hair and turned his back on me. "You're tired, you need to rest. You should sit down. You've been through a lot," he said quickly. I arched an eyebrow, surprised at his reaction. Evidently not every member of the Howlers was aggressive, but I was intrigued by his words. I decided to return to the couch and folded my legs underneath me. I kept my voice low and soft, and spoke slowly. I remembered what Jack had said about songs being a spell able to enchant people, and while I didn't want to give anything he said any credence, I did try and think about the way I could use my voice and body language to manipulate Matt.

"What did you mean by 'it isn't time'? Time for what exactly?"

Matt licked his lips and chewed the bottom one nervously. He paced the floor before me.

"How was your walk with Jack last night?" he asked.

"It was fine. Although he's somewhat mysterious and a little frightening, and his grip is hard," I said, rubbing my arm. A little fear crept into my voice as I remembered the way he held me. Matt looked at me with concern and walked over. He pulled my sleeve up and looked at my arm and then cursed under his breath.

"Was this Jack?" he asked.

I nodded.

"I'm sorry," he said in a long breath. "I'm sorry for all of this."

"Then at least you can tell me what it's about. I've been going stir crazy not knowing what you're going to do to me, just waiting for the worst to happen. I don't like being at the mercy of dangerous men, Matt, and if you're going to do something awful then I wish you would just get on with it already. It's bad enough that you had to bring me here against my will, but then you're cruel enough to leave me to stew in my own worry. I'm losing my mind, Matt. It's only been one night and I'm already going crazy." I reached out and placed my hand on his arm, squeezing it gently. "Please tell me," I begged.

I could feel his resolve weakening, like a dam that burst under a torrent of water. He tried to resist. He stood up and walked away, putting distance between us, but I could tell that, against all odds, he had a good heart. His regret was genuine and I could sense that he really wanted to help me, that he really believed he'd had no choice, and if that was the case then I could try and turn it to my advantage.

"What did Jack tell you?" he asked.

"Not much really. He told me some story about the moon and then complimented me on my singing, said something about how magic did exist in the world and singing was an example of that. Frankly it didn't make much sense."

"I see."

"Do you? Because I don't."

Matt exhaled deeply. "I can't tell you anything until Jack decides it's time. I'm sorry."

My eyes darkened. "Matt, please, I'm going out of my mind with worry. All I want is something to hold onto, something that might make a little sense out of all of this. There's so much that I don't understand. Why did you kidnap me in the first place? Why me out of all the others? Just tell me, please, and if you don't, then just give me one of those magic potions you come up with and knock me out again. I'd rather be asleep than have to deal with all of this."

Matt smiled wryly. "They're not magic potions, they're just blends of natural herbs and flowers that have different effects. It's a skill that was passed down to me from my mother," he said. I nodded, acting interested even though I didn't really care all that much.

"So can you make me another one to knock me out so I can be at peace? I can see there's no point in me fighting. I might as well just sleep and you can do whatever you want with me. I know I'm going to end up dead anyway...I just wish you would all get it over with," my voice trailed away as I got to the end of the sentence and pure sadness came through. This whole situation was so difficult and there were moments when there was nothing in my mind but bleak despair. I was certain there was no way out for me; they might as well just have drugged me up and used me like some kind of doll. At least if I was out of my mind I wouldn't have to deal with any of it.

I started to wonder if, actually, Mom had been my tether to the world all along. Once the flame of her life was extinguished there was no place for me in the world and fate had to correct the imbalance. If my life was an aberration then perhaps it was time for me to die after all. I just hoped that when it came, it came quickly.

But Matt reacted horribly to me saying that. He gasped in shock and shook his head dramatically, raising his hands in surrender.

"That's not what's going on here at all. We don't want to put you in danger Trish. We don't want to hurt you." He seemed genuinely wounded that I would ever think otherwise.

"Then why did you bring me here?" I asked, my voice almost a growl. I glared at Matt and I could see him wilting. He looked to the closed door and he swallowed his nerves.

"I can't tell you everything. That's Jack's place. But I can tell you that you are special. You might not believe, but..." he blinked for a few moments and collected his thoughts. "There is a lot of history in the world and there have been a lot of dynasties. Some of them have purer bloodlines than others. You are the result of one of these bloodlines and we need you to make us strong again..." he trailed off. I looked at him with my head tilted to the side, and then I threw my head back and laughed.

"You think my bloodline is pure? Mine?" I almost collapsed on the couch at the thought. If mine was one of the few pure bloodlines in existence then the human race was in more trouble than I thought. "I think you've made a mistake."

"There can be no mistake," Matt stated. My laughter died as I noticed the terse way he spoke and how his jaw was clenched. He fully believed in what he was saying and I finally realized that I was in the grip of a cult. The color drained from my face. The talk of making the group strong again...that could mean only one thing...breeding.

My mind caved in on itself when I thought about the ramifications. They wanted to take my body away from me, take away my choice and use me as some kind of vessel for their entire group, to bring forth a new generation of, what, bikers? It seemed too ridiculous to be true, and the way Matt acted made it seem as though it was the most important thing in the world. I thought back to the previous night and to Jack...he was evidently their leader and his mind wasn't in the right place. He spoke of so many strange things. Oh God...what had I gotten myself into? I had to escape, and as soon as possible. I couldn't stay there and let them breed me, with this strange talk of a bloodline. What could they possibly know about my bloodline? I was just an ordinary girl who had been a failure in life. There wasn't anything special about me, and I wasn't about to let their misunderstanding ruin me. I wasn't going to be used to breed their children in some kind of weird cult.

I shuddered and nausea churned in the pit of my stomach. My skin crawled with revulsion at the thought of being taken and used for this horrid purpose, my body just a tool for one single purpose. My heart sank and the world seemed to blur around me, when I realized that tears had filled my eyes. But now was not the time for sadness. I had to try and make my escape. I had to try and be strong for a little longer. I wiped my eyes and inhaled deeply, in an attempt to keep myself composed.

"That's...that's a lot to take in Matt," I said softly. He relaxed when I stopped laughing. "I'm sorry for laughing. I just didn't know how to react."

He walked over to me and took my hand, placing it between his palms. "I'm sorry that I can't tell you more. I promise that you will understand before too long, you just have to be patient with us. But this isn't a bad thing Trish. In fact it's quite wonderful. You'll see, I promise."

"I hope you're right," I squeezed his palm to try and make more of an impression on him, and then I rose from the couch and pressed my hand against the wall. "I just feel like I'm losing my mind in here. There's so much to take in. I want to understand all of this, but I can't concentrate. I dread going back to that cell, Matt," I turned to him with desperation in my eyes, "please can we go for a walk first? I enjoyed being outside with Jack last night, but it was so dark I didn't get to appreciate the surroundings properly. I just...it would calm me to be out in nature, to feel the warmth of the sun on my skin and the grass underneath my feet."

Matt shifted his gaze away, unsure of my request. He stroked his chin. "I don't know..." he said.

"I promise I'll be good," I smiled sweetly, "and you'll be there. I know that nothing will happen while you're there." I knew that Matt wouldn't pull me back like Jack did. Taking advantage of Matt's kindness was the only weapon I had in my arsenal. "Just for a little while, just so I get a better grip of my sanity. You don't know what it's like to go through all this..." I said.

The tug on his heart strings seemed to work.

"Okay, but just for a little while, just so you can get some exercise," he said. "But don't stray too far and don't try anything," he jabbed a finger towards me and I nodded obediently, but his words did not carry the same hissing threat that Jack's had. My eyes gleamed as I followed him outside, because I knew I had a chance to escape this awful hell.

Chapter Six

Bathed in sunlight, the world was even more beautiful than it had been at night. The green meadow stretched out all around us, leading to a lush forest. The trees beckoned with their tempting shade and the branches swayed in the breeze, the leaves whispering for us to join them. The blue sky was dotted with wispy clouds, but these weren't enough to block out the sun, which burned with a radiant light. Beyond the trees were red mountains, their summits jagged and harsh, turning to grey as they rose up, pointing to the heavens. Birds soared above and I envied them their freedom. The long road stretched out with not a soul upon it. The Howlers had chosen a fine spot for their motorcycle club. It was far away from anything and anyone, a forgotten part of the world where secrets could easily be kept.

When I commented on this, Matt looked rueful.

"There was a town a few miles that way," he pointed to the road that seemed to stretch to nowhere, "that was where the Howlers lived along with the rest of the folk, but over time it's become a ghost town. People have moved to the city. There wasn't much left for them out here once the world changed and things got all modern and evolved," there was evident disdain in his voice. "Now we just all stay in the clubhouse."

"Sounds like it could get crowded."

Matt shrugged. "It's okay. If we ever need alone time we can ride. When we're on a bike the whole world is open to us," he said.

"As long as you have a road ahead of you," I replied, smirking. Matt tilted his head and nodded. The way they lived was far from the way I was used to living. They were a small group, a relic of a time that didn't fit into the modern way of the world. It was no wonder that their numbers had dwindled since people had moved on to bigger and better things, easier things. A place like this was a place lost to time, and it attracted people with a certain worldview, or people who had nothing waiting for them elsewhere. They were outcasts and, in a way, I thought that, actually, I might fit in quite nicely.

But I wasn't going to be anyone's breeding pet.

I suppose I could imagine well how such an idea might take place. Out here, far from the world it was easy to believe that they were above the law and that the normal rules of the world didn't apply to them. They could come up with their own schemes and their own plans. I imagined there was much frustration from the fact that their numbers had dwindled, and if recruiting didn't work, then what other way was there to get new members other than having their own? I doubted that I was the last girl they'd try this with. I guessed I was the test run. Maybe they'd overhead me talking to Rachel about my Mom and realized that I had nothing in the world, so I was an easy target. I was so distraught that night I probably didn't realize that they were close to me, listening and stalking, waiting for that moment to strike. It was a crazed world and it was scary to think that people could be brought to this way of thinking when they were so far removed from anything normal. I'd seen a lot of crazy things in life, and at that point I knew that if I made it out of there alive I'd have a damned good story to tell.

I started walking towards the forest, testing Matt's reaction.

"Hey, where are you going?" he cried out. I stopped, but I didn't turn around. I merely twisted my head and tossed a gaze over my shoulder, my eyes barely visible through my veil of hair.

"I was heading to the forest, for a stroll," I said.

"No, we'd better stay close to the clubhouse. I don't think it's a good idea to go too far. You just needed a short walk. There's plenty of space here." He gestured around at the meadow and he was right, but there wasn't enough cover for me to hide in and there weren't shadows that would allow my escape. I started walking towards the forest, taking small strides to ensure that he didn't react hastily.

"I need to get out of the sun. The forest will offer some shade. I'll only go to the edge. The plants look more interesting there anyway. I was hoping that you could teach me something about them. I've never been interested in flowers," I said. "How did your Mom teach you?"

Playing on his interest worked, as he skipped up to me and warned me that we'd only be going to the edge. I smirked, as my plan was coming to fruition. I needed to get away from the prying eyes of the clubhouse and then make my move. If I got into the forest then I was one step closer to home or, frankly, anywhere away from here. I didn't care where I ended up, just as long as it was far away from this crazy place.

"She used to bring me out here and she taught me about how different herbs and plants go together. So one might be harmful when it is by itself, but paired with something else it has a different effect entirely. Some are used to treat wounds, some can induce sleep, some are nourishing. The natural world gives us a lot and we don't use it to its full potential. The knowledge that has been passed down to me is valuable and there's a danger of it getting lost. The way the world is now...people don't have the time or patience to learn skills like these. It's an art, and I'm not bragging by saying that."

"I'm sure you're not," I said, and I got him to pick out a few things. We reached the edge of the forest. He was happily chatting away. I glanced over my shoulder as the clubhouse receded into the distance and I was glad that nobody had noticed our absence or, if they had, they had enough confidence in Matt to handle me. The shadows touched our bodies and the air grew cooler. Now that we were out of the sun my skin prickled as the temperature changed. Green light bathed us as the leaves shielded us from the sun and the world smelled earthy and genuine.

"What was she like, your Mom?" I asked, as we walked deeper and deeper into the woods, betraying his intention to keep to the edge. The shadows enveloped us and I had him alone, so I felt more confident of succeeding in my goals. He picked up a few flowers here and there, or pointed out an herb and told me about it. I filed away the information for later, but I was mostly concerned with getting my bearings and looking for the best way out. Thankfully there were a lot of fallen branches on the ground and I just had to wait for the right moment, and it had to be right. If I acted at the wrong time it would ruin any chance I had of escaping. Matt would never trust me again and I'd never be allowed out on a walk in the forest.

"Oh she was wonderful, so kind and caring. Dad was away a lot so she brought me up mostly by herself. But she taught me all about the world and what it meant to be a part of the balance. She said that everything had a purpose in the world, even if it was really small, and that one day I'd find my purpose. The knowledge of these plants had been passed down for generations and I was happy to learn. Sometimes we'd spend entire weeks camping out here, learning all about the natural world. People thought we were strange, but we were happy."

"It sounds peaceful, and nice that you were so close," I said, feeling a little envious that he had such a close relationship with his Mom when mine had been so fractious. "What made you want to join the MC then? Didn't you want to take this knowledge elsewhere? Maybe you could have started your own school and taught others, spread the knowledge a bit?"

A rueful look came upon his face.

"I couldn't leave the MC. It's in my blood. As much as the world has moved on, I couldn't leave. It's my destiny."

"You sound like you believe all that stuff," I folded my arms across my chest.

"You will too, once you understand everything. It's...there's something bigger out there than all of us and it binds us together. It sets us on a path and we have to do our best to keep to that. There's a chain that remains unbroken between all that live, and we are but links. The only purpose we have in life is to ensure that the chain continues."

"Did your mother teach you that?"

"No, my father did, actually."

"Even though he was away a lot?"

"He came back when he could and he was away on important business. Did you know your father?" Matt asked pointedly. Breath caught in my throat, as rarely anyone asked me about my father.

"No, I didn't," I said curtly. "It was always just me and Mom. She said that he was some actor and she was trying to get on his show, but he never repaid the promise he made and instead of a life in show business she had me instead."

"It was a good trade," Matt said.

I smiled at the kind words. "Not for her. As far as she was concerned, I had taken away any chance she had of being famous. She blamed me for it, and tried to redeem that one mistake by giving me the life she never had, but I wasn't her. I couldn't be her. I couldn't do the things she wanted me to do and it all ended in failure."

"I don't know about that, you sang beautifully on stage. I'm sure if you really wanted it you could have been famous."

"But that was the issue, I never really wanted it and Mom couldn't understand why. To her fame was all that mattered."

"Aside from you. She gave it all up for you."

"I don't think she had much of a choice."

"People always have a choice and she chose you. You were her choice, even if she never fully accepted the way her life turned out and, maybe, you were just meant for something greater," he said.

I hated to admit it, but talking to Matt was good for my soul. Nobody had ever said anything with such clarity before and he made me see Mom in a different light. I never really thought about what it must have been like for her to be faced with the impossible choice of having a child or having another shot at the career she had always dreamed of having. She had thrown that all away for my sake and, I suppose, I shouldn't have been too angry at her for trying to force me into the Hollywood life, as it was the only thing she knew. Just like

Matt's mother she had tried to pass on her knowledge and, like a brat, I had only thought of myself and never realized what it truly meant.

And I'd never get the chance to tell her.

"I guess it doesn't matter now anyway. She's dead and I'm here," I said. The mood darkened and suddenly things had taken an unexpected turn. I hadn't prepared to share any of my innermost feelings with one of these men and I had to hold my heart together to stop it from falling apart and ruining my chances of escaping. My mind whirred as Matt continued talking about some of the history of the MC, how his father had proudly worn the badge and how, even though Matt hadn't seen him that much, he still wanted to emulate the man. It was a good thing for someone to have such a close connection with his parents and it made me realize how bereft I had been of family guidance. Whenever I thought of my father there was nothing but a blank slate, an empty space where a person should have been. Mom never told me anything about him either. I had tried to do some detective work and figure out which show he had been working on when Mom had the relationship, but I'd never made any progress. When I was a kid I used to dream that one day he'd track me down, that he wanted to find me as much as I wanted to find him and in some strange way our two fates would collide, drawn together by an invisible string that was unbreakable.

But it never happened.

"My word," Matt suddenly gasped. He crouched down near a plant with black leaves, shaped like lapels on a shirt. He spoke in a hushed tone, as though the plant was prey and it would run away if he spoke loudly. He curled his hands around it protectively and the plant seemed to react to his presence, the petals twitched. "Now this is one of the rarest plants found in the wood. I've barely seen it bloom and you might be quite interested in this one because when distilled and paired with-"

But I didn't get to hear what the effects would be, nor did I care. As soon as he crouched down and his back was turned to me I searched around for a weapon, knowing that this was my chance. I was far enough into the woods that I could get a good head start before Matt awoke and raised the alarm. I might even be able to flee and escape this hell, and get back to the fragments of my real life. As he marveled at the plant, his attention completely enraptured by the black leaves, I curled my hand around a thick branch. I felt a little guilty at first, as he had been nice to me and shared his emotions with me. He'd even gotten me to open up and talk about my deep feelings, as well as reflect on things that I hadn't thought about for a while. But I hardened my heart and reminded myself that even if he was the nicest of the three, he had still been a part of a trio that had kidnapped me and that was unforgivable. I wasn't going to give myself to them. I wasn't going to meekly surrender to this breeding wish of theirs. Mom had always taught me how to fight, and if that was the only legacy she had left me, then it was a worthy one.

I screamed as I swung the branch. It caught Matt right in the temple. The branch cracked and splintered as it hit him, and he went down like he had been shot. His body sprawled over the ground, and the impact had made him pinch the plant up from the roots. It rested in his hand. He moaned softly and his head lolled to the side. There was no blood, and I was almost certain that I hadn't killed him, but I wasn't going to stick around to find out.

I dropped the branch and turned on my heels, sprinting away. My muscles began to ache almost immediately. I wasn't the fittest person in the world at the best of times and I had been through quite an ordeal already, but I fought the throbbing pain, hurtling through the forest as quickly as I could. I thought my best bet was to keep within the forest as long as I could, and then to go through the mountains. If I found the road then it would be easier for them to track me down. In the wilderness there was no chance of them finding me, the only danger I had was from nature itself, and a lack of food and water, but I was free. I was free! Elation ran through my heart as the branches whipped my face and skin, but I didn't care. The lashing pain reminded me that I was alive, that I still had a say in my destiny.

Chapter Seven

My throat ached. Every breath was like swallowing shattered glass as I yearned to slake my thirst. The forest seemed to be unending. The trees were all the same and I had long lost my bearings. I ran ahead, although I had turned to the side as trees had gotten in my way. Occasionally there was a break in the leaves and shards of sunlight burst through, hitting me with a warm glow. I stumbled over fallen logs, but I didn't let them stop me. I dared not look behind me for fear that I would see one of them chasing after me, hunting me. The fine hairs on the back of my neck stood up with a dread feeling that there was something coming after me. The day was still light, but I feared the approach of the night when all kinds of dark creatures would come out of the shadows.

I stopped whenever I found a brook or a stream, which wasn't frequent enough for my liking. I dared not stop for too long though, so I nourished myself on handfuls of water before I left again. I had no way to carry water, so I had to live in hope that I would find another one before my body surrendered. Fruit and berries hung from trees. I was wary of some of the berries and wished that I had asked Matt about them before I had left him, and I left my stomach to rumble. Insects buzzed about me and a few small animals scurried about. I swear that at one point I heard a snake slithering by, but I decided to not let my fear get the better of me.

I continued on, driven to escape the forest and work my way around the mountain, hoping that there was something else on the other side, something that led to civilization. All I needed was for one truck to see me and I could escape, I could flee and tell the police about what had happened.

Then I could hide for the rest of my life.

There were plenty of other people who had survived on nature and I told myself that I still could last a few days without food or water. As long as I had a little shelter during the night I would be fine, and I'd feel better once I was confident that nobody was going to find me.

I knew that I was a part of a wider world. I knew that out there, there were cities filled with masses of people and millions of souls, each living their own lives. I knew that there were whole industries churning along, a whole society with its laws and rules and boundaries...but as I ran through the forest I felt alone. I might as well have been the only person in the entire world, except for the three men who had kidnapped me. I couldn't shake the feeling that if they had found me once they could find me again. No amount of steps seemed to be enough to escape their reach and I started to wonder about life if I escaped. Would I have to move somewhere else and change my name, or even leave the country? My entire life would have to change because of this. I couldn't believe that it had only been one night. It felt like a lifetime ago when I was in the bar with Rachel, lamenting the state of the world.

I staggered along and eventually I had to give up and rest. My legs were screaming and as soon as I stopped I sank onto the ground and heaved in heavy breaths. I gulped in air as though it was water and let my body enjoy some ease. The glade was filled with soft grass and I lay down, knowing that I needed to rest if I was to continue on my journey. The need to soothe my aching muscles overrode my fear of being caught. I must have put enough distance between myself and them now to be confident of an escape. I figured I had at least an hour before Matt awoke, perhaps even longer, and then he'd have to go back to the clubhouse and tell the others. Then they'd have to scour the forest, not knowing in which direction I'd gone. I breathed a little easier as I thought it through and it became clear to me that they wouldn't be able to catch up.

As far as I was concerned I was completely free and there was no chance of them finding me. I breathed a little easier and a smile crept upon my face. I thought to the future. Part of me just wanted to leave this all behind and not even think about it again, but I knew that if I didn't come forward other women might be at risk. I couldn't let that happen. I would expose them for what they were and the hammer of justice would slam down upon their heads. I would be a hero and, ironically, it might even catapult me to the fame that Mom had always wanted for me. Everyone loved a true crime story. I was certain that I'd be interviewed for all the daily talk shows and I might even have a book or a Hollywood movie made out of my ordeal. Maybe Scarlett Johansson could play me...what a dream.

Mom would probably say that the trauma was all worth it if something like that came out of it. What a cruel joke fate was. This is why I didn't like to believe in anything grander than mere chance pulling my life along, for if there was such a thing as fate then it had a malevolent sense of humor.

I was so exhausted that I probably could have stayed there for the rest of the day. My legs were heavy and my mind was dazed. My clothes clung to my body with uncomfortable sweat, but I knew if I stayed there I would lose all the advantages I had gained. I pushed myself up with a groan and continued forward, ignoring the lancing pain in my legs. The loneliness was getting to me though and I couldn't shake the feeling that something was watching me. I glanced around. Shadows danced, but I saw no other person, yet I couldn't get rid of this feeling.

So I started to sing.

My voice was not nearly as pure as it had been on stage, since it was bleeding with desperate breaths, but hearing an actual sound calmed me. I sang some of Mom's old favorites. I kept my voice soft and low in the hope that it wouldn't travel far and give my position away.

*

I had been walking for the better part of the day and was just about ready to drop when I suddenly heard a sound that chilled me to the bone. I stopped singing and the air went quiet around me, apart from some rustling in the trees, and it was more rustling than what a simple breeze could cause. My chest tightened and fear crawled like ice down my throat. My pace slowed. They couldn't have caught up with me could they? I retraced my steps and thought about everything I had done, wondering if I should have pushed myself harder, or taken another path. I glanced behind me, trying to see if I had left a trail of footsteps lodged in the ground, but there was nothing there. I wracked my brains to figure out how they had found me, when suddenly a grim conclusion came to my mind.

If it wasn't them, it was something else. Something dangerous.

A hunter.

I gulped as I continued moving, hoping that it was simply my mind playing tricks on me and there wasn't actually anything to be worried about. My furtive gaze darted all around me, trying to parse the woodland for the threat I was certain lay in wait, but I could see nothing. Still, some primal instinct told me that I was in danger.

I started to run. As my body moved into a sprint I saw a black shape move to my left. It circled around, and then suddenly a wolf broke through the forest before me. Branches cracked and leaves were ripped away. The wolf, bigger than any I had seen before, loomed above me. Its teeth were so white, stark against its black fur. Its eyes were beady and dark, and it stared at me with death. A low growl rumbled like thunder and I crawled back, searching for a way out, but two more wolves accompanied it, both of them as black as night. I shook my head and pressed myself against a tree. I clutched at the trunk for safety, and clawed at it, trying to climb it to at least escape their grasp, hoping that I could wait them out, even though they looked strong enough to uproot a tree entirely.

I groaned as I glanced over my shoulder and looked at them coming towards me. I could see the desire in their eyes, wanting to tear me apart. Tears cascaded down my cheeks as I was completely helpless. I had gone from one bad situation to another, and from this there was no escape. I meekly surrendered in tears, falling to my knees and bowing my head. I closed my eyes and prayed that it would be over quickly.

And then there was a howl.

I looked up, fearful of more wolves, but these were different. One was huge, bigger than all the others, with grey fur covering sinewy muscles. Another was tawny brown, lithe and fierce. The one that came charging in with the most ferocity and passion was a white wolf. He was lean and mean, every muscle in his body seemed primed for combat. His ears were flat against his head and his black nose was pointed forward. His jaws were opened and they hissed death. The three ran in like a blur, thundering around me. I held up my hands around my head and screamed, trembled, wishing that the world would swallow me up and take me away from this forsaken place. I turned and watched the whirlwind of wolves as they sought battle with each other. The black wolves turned their attention away from me and formed a defensive posture. The white wolf ran forward, ahead of his two allies, snarling with bestial fury. He threw himself in between two of the black wolves and they went tumbling around, their tails twisting and the fur blending into a blurred vision of violence.

The bigger grey wolf crashed in like a tank. He went straight for the remaining black wolf, butting heads. The black wolf lost its balance and fell with a whimper. The grey wolf slashed and clawed. Blood spurt out in a crimson wave. The tawny brown wolf did not fight. It stood in front of me, acting like a shield between me and the violence. It didn't make sense at the time. Was this how wolves behaved?

The white wolf yapped and bit at the two wolves around him. The tumult was so chaotic that, at first, he seemed to have the advantage. He tore flesh and fur away from the wolves and the forest was alive with the yelps of pain and the growls of fury. The initial advantage had been taken away though. Once the black wolves regained their footing they asserted themselves and swiped at the white wolf. Jaws snapped, powerful enough to crunch through bone. I gasped at such a display of animal strength. It was more intense than anything I had witnessed before and I feared for my life. I tried to move, but I was paralyzed with terror. There was nothing I could do but watch.

The white wolf wriggled and squirmed to try and assert his dominance again, but it seemed as though he had acted too rashly. He gave as good as he got, but the two big black wolves seemed intent on destroying him. They tore a chunk of flesh out of his shoulder, which sent him staggering back. If I had been the white wolf I would have retreated, but the vicious animal was relentless and would not give any quarter. Even though he was wounded he snapped back at them and tried to fight. The tawny brown wolf growled and I wondered if he was going to join in to defend his brethren, but he didn't need to. The grey wolf howled loudly as he charged in and stood next to the white wolf, bringing his huge paw down in a vicious swipe that cut the black wolf along the side of the face. The black wolf yelped in pain and now the odds had suddenly changed. With one of them dead already and with the huge grey wolf standing alongside the white it seemed as though they had little chance, even though I could sense some of the power that surged through their bodies.

They snarled and backed away as the grey and white wolves reared their bodies ready to strike out. I could almost see the moment when they realized that things hadn't gone the way they had planned. They backed away, and took their terrible anger with them. The three wolves howled in unison as a final warning cry to the black wolves that they had won.

They had won me.

Fear gripped my soul as I realized that I had just substituted three wolves for three more. I pressed myself tightly against the tree and moaned, shaking my head as the wolves turned towards me. They panted because of the vigor of battle and slowly turned their beady gazes upon me. Breath caught in my throat and I wasn't sure what to think when suddenly I locked eyes with the white wolf. I knew those eyes.

They were golden.

Chapter Eight

I didn't understand how it was possible at the time, but those eyes were the same eyes as I had seen when I had awoken during the ride away from the bar. I thought that it had been a simple trick of the mind, and even at this moment I was still convinced that something was wrong. After all, I was exhausted and flooded with fear. My mind was in complete disarray. Then it happened. I'm not even sure how to describe it. The wolves stepped towards me and I thought they were going to take me as their prey, that this had all been some battle over a piece of flesh and I was going to be their dinner. My heart shifted from hope to despair and I believed that whatever respite I had been given it was only a temporary one, but then the air shimmered around the wolves. Their bodies started to shift. Fur receded and they reared back on their hind legs. Their faces flattened and took on human features. The whole process looked as though it must have hurt, but the men bore it with a stoic quality and then, by some miracle, there were no longer three wolves standing before me, but three men. Jack, Buck, and Matt.

I blinked and rubbed my eyes, but that was the moment when I started to believe in the impossible.

*

I'd barely had a chance to process the information when Jack stormed forward and tugged me up.

"I told you not to run away! Do you have any idea what they would have done to you?" he raged. His face was like thunder and he glared at me. His hand was rough again. He held me like he owned me.

"Don't treat her like that! She's been through a lot. You should be gentler," Matt said, rushing in to my defense, even though I had hurt him.

"Oh don't get me started, Matt," Jack turned and scowled, not letting go of me. "This wouldn't have happened if you had just listened to me. I told you to keep her inside. We almost lost everything because of you." Matt was silenced.

"This whole thing is trouble. I told you from the beginning. There's no way the Hunters were going to let us get away with this. We should have attacked them from the outset, reminded them who's boss," Buck folded his arms and didn't seem to care about me at all. He barely looked in my direction and seemed more concerned with facing into the distance, towards the direction in which these Hunters had run. While the three bickered I wondered if I was ever going to get a chance to speak. I wrestled my arm away from Jack's grip, which would only make it bruise even more, and pulled myself away.

Jack looked shocked that I would even dare try to escape.

"Whatever they would have done to me wouldn't have been any worse than what you're doing," I said sullenly.

Jack laughed, but it was a laugh that was completely devoid of humor. "You have no idea what you're talking about," he spat.

"No, I don't, because you won't tell me anything," I shot back, glaring at him. My emotions ran wild and my entire body bristled with manic energy. I trembled with anguish, angry that I had been so close to escaping only to have the chance snatched away from me. At least I knew how they had tracked me though. With the nose of a wolf it would have been easy to track my path. God, when I looked at them I could barely believe they had just transformed from wolves. What the hell was I doing? I was certain that I had to have been hallucinating, but everything else seemed entirely real and I could do nothing but go with the flow and hope that somehow this would all end up making sense.

"We should tell her Jack. It's not going to do any good keeping the truth from her, not now that she's seen this. She was going to find out anyway. Maybe once she knows she'll understand better," Matt said.

Jack turned away and breathed deeply, closing his eyes for a moment as he tried to calm the energy within.

"What you're about to learn has been a secret for a long time, for generations in fact. I would have preferred to wait for you to learn about our story, but I suppose it cannot be helped now. You should sit down. This may take some time," he began. I glanced towards Matt, who looked away from me. Buck scanned the horizon to ensure that nothing disturbed us. I did as Jack asked and sank to the ground, eager to finally hear his tale and shed some light on what the hell was going on.

*

"It all started a long time ago," Jack began. "I tried to tell you last night that there are greater forces in the world, but you wouldn't listen. I needed you to have more of an open mind before I told you all of this, but now I have no choice, so I hope that you take everything I say in good faith. Nobody quite knows how werewolves came into existence, but the fact is we have been a part of the world for a long time, as long as humans. But there have always been few of us. We have kept track of the bloodlines through the years to ensure that our brood remains pure. Our packs require excellent breeding to remain strong and for years the system was flawless. But then the world began to change. There were more opportunities calling to people, seducing people. The world became a bigger place and suddenly members of the pack wanted to leave to pursue other things. The numbers dwindled and the fear is that we'd start to lose our way of life. The fewer of us there are, the harder it is to repopulate. The werewolf gene is recessive. If we were to mate with a human it would be lost. We need someone borne of a wolf bloodline to breed with," he said.

"But that...that doesn't make any sense. I'm not of a wolf bloodline. I'm just a regular girl."

"No, you're not. Your father was a wolf," Jack said.

I gulped. "No. how do you know?"

"He was one of us, but he died. The wolves that found you are called the Hunters. They have been our rivals for a number of years now and will do anything to stop us. They killed him. One by one they have been hunting us over the years, trying to take our place as the most powerful pack. They have been hunting you too, trying to keep you from us. Trust me, they would have done far worse things to you," Jack said.

My mind reeled. I could barely believe what he was saying.

"No...no...this doesn't make sense. This is all too much. It's just crazy."

Jack sighed and turned to the others. "I told you she wasn't ready. What's the point in telling her when she's not ready to believe?"

"She will believe, she just needs time," Matt said.

"She'll only try and escape again. We need to keep her chained up this time," Buck snarled.

"No, wait," I said, hating that they were talking about me as though I wasn't even there. "I just need time to understand. How can this be possible? How can you even exist?"

"Is it so hard to believe that such a thing is possible when there are so many other miracles that occur every day? Nobody knows for certain why we have been given this gift, it is just the way things are. But you have seen it for your own eyes. There is no use in disbelieving. Only acceptance can set you free."

"And my father?"

"His name was Jake. He was one of the best of us. He was our leader for a time. He met your mother, but the Hunters got to him before anything could happen. They knew he was seeing someone, and they wanted to know because his offspring would be desirable, either a powerful male wolf or a pure female carrying the wolf gene. There has always been a tradition where the females carry the wolf heritage. We believe it's from Mother Moon. Your father did not tell them who your mother was, so none of us knew, but then at the bar when you started singing I knew that it could be no other. In your song you carry the legacy of the wolves, and after we met you it was clear. You are his child. You can be our future. Your place is here with us. It is what he would have wanted."

It was so much for me to take in. I had no idea how I was supposed to process it all. I had never known anything of my father, and now I was suddenly being given so much information it was difficult for me to handle.

Jack leaned down. His breath was warm and sweet. "I know you do not understand, but we must take you back. Your place is with us. The future of our pack relies on you," he said. I was so numb that I could do nothing but nod in reply and be led up by his hand. We walked back to the clubhouse and it didn't seem to take nearly as long as it had taken me to flee, but perhaps that was because my mind whirled at a million miles an hour, struggling to understand my place in the world and how everything fit together.

*

We were back in the small room where I had started the day with Matt. Jack pointed to a picture on the wall.

"That's him," he said. I peered at the faded photograph, at the man who was purportedly my father. He was tall and broad-shouldered. He had a leather jacket on and a round helmet upon his head. A handlebar moustache was thick, and he certainly seemed the type Mom would go for. He smiled widely and his eyes twinkled with delight. Surrounding him were the other members of the MC, or the pack, looking so happy as though nothing could harm them. My gaze drifted to the next photo, one in which he was absent. The smiles were gone from the faces and there were fewer people. Clouds gathered in the distance as though a great storm was rising.

"Mom never told me..."

"She didn't know. He wouldn't have told her. I'm sure he intended to, but the Hunters got to him," Jack said, leaning against the table with his arms folded across his chest and he looked somber.

"What beef do they have with you?" I asked.

"They're just jealous. They think they're stronger, so they want to take us out. They're younger, arrogant, and they think they're deserving of the purer bloodline. They'd stop at nothing to get you. That's why I had to keep you like that, so they couldn't get to you."

"You could have told me," I pouted.

"Would you have believed me? I can see it in your eyes that you barely believe it now. Even after you've seen things for yourself, you still struggle. What use would it have been for me to tell you all of this?"

I had nothing to say to that. A cold shiver ran down my spine as I thought on his words and about the other world that existed between these packs, a world that had been hidden from me. I was the first to admit that there was much about the world I didn't know, but this was almost too much to believe. Yet what alternative did I have? I had seen them shift with my own eyes, and everything they said made sense. When I looked at the picture of my father I saw myself in his eyes. I could almost feel a spiritual connection to him...but how could I open my heart and mind to this when it seemed so alien and distant?

"Where do we go from here?" I asked softly.

"We'll keep you safe. Matt has a plan. Something to help you understand properly. Try not to hit him around the head this time. I'm sure it was an accident before," Jack snapped as he marched out of the room. Matt came in swiftly after him and looked reserved. Pangs of guilt stabbed at my heart, even though I felt justified in what I did. But Matt had been the only one to be kind to me.

"Have you come to terms with everything Jack told you?" Matt asked.

"Not quite. It's a lot to take in. Matt I'm...I'm sorry about before. Surely you can understand why I did what I did? It wasn't personal. I just needed to try. What you've done to me is wrong, even if what Jack said is right and that you were doing this to protect me. You should have told me all of this from the beginning."

"Jack said it wouldn't have made any difference. He said that with patience you would come around, and we're used to trusting his judgment around here. I thought we should tell you and I hoped that you'd be patient enough to understand. I guess I kind of hoped that being here would spark something inside you considering you're Jake's daughter, but I think that was too much to hope for. I've come up with something that might help you though."

"What is it?" I asked curiously, kind of intrigued to know how I might be able to learn more about my past and understand everything that was being told to me from a trusted source, without having to just take Jack's word on everything. While he clearly believed what he was saying I didn't know how I could trust him, given everything that had happened so far. How could I give him my trust when he had taken me from my life without any concern for my wishes? And he didn't trust me enough to tell me the truth...maybe he was correct in that respect considering that I still couldn't comprehend the truth of the matter even though I had seen it with my own eyes.

My word...the image of the beasts turning into men made me wonder if I had always been crazy. It was so unreal, and yet I had seen it with my own eyes. I had heard their growls turn into words. I had seen the fur recede into their bodies and be left with flesh. I had witnessed the magic swirling around them, a deep part of this world that I had never been aware of before. How was anyone supposed to understand this kind of thing? I struggled to know where to turn from here. I needed some kind of guidance. I clearly couldn't escape, and even if I did escape I had no idea how I would be able to leave this behind. How could I go through life when knowing that these secrets were held in the world? No, I had to stay here and try to figure this out. If there was a mystery to the world, then I was going to get to the bottom of it and, in doing so, maybe I would unravel the mystery of my father as well.

"Actually it's something that I was going to explain to you before you hit me," Matt said. There was an undercurrent of tension to his voice.

"I'm sorry about that, I..." I stammered out again.

"You have to understand Trish; there are people here who aren't against you. I know it might not seem like it, but there are those of us who genuinely care."

"Like Buck?" I challenged. Matt smiled.

"Buck is Buck," he said. "I mean people like me. I never wanted to hurt you like this and I wish we could have been straight with you from the beginning, but surely you can understand why we had to do what we did. I want you to try and think of things from our perspective, and maybe this will help with that." He pulled out a dark liquid. It was as though he had distilled the essence of night and poured it into a glass. I instantly shuddered and reeled back at the sight of it, some instinctive part of me told me that it wasn't right. From the look on Matt's face I could tell that was an accurate assumption.

"What is this?" I asked, with caution in my voice.

"This is the product of the rare plant I found before you left. It's known as the Styx plant, because it bridges this world and the next."

"When you say the next..." I almost couldn't dare to imagine what he meant.

"Trish, it's important that you start to believe in a world beyond your own. When spirits die they go to another realm. This plant allows your mind to float up and talk with spirits that have departed this world. Don't ask me how it works; I only know that it does. I have spoken with my own mother thanks to this plant. With this you can speak to your mother and your father, if they are willing. It might help you understand us a little more, and come to terms with your place in this world."

He held out the glass. The liquid was thick and looked like oil. Even if I believed that this was possible I wasn't sure I wanted to speak to my mother again...but how could I pass up the opportunity? There was conflict in my mind and when I didn't take it Matt left it on the table. The liquid sat there, but it had a hold on me. Whispers coiled around the back of my mind and tempted me, told me to take the chance because it was the only one I might get at understanding all of this.

Then the door opened and Matt was called out by Buck. The large wolf stood there, filling up the doorway. Matt glared.

"Leave us alone Buck," Matt said.

"Jack wants to speak to you. I'll watch the girl," he said.

I scowled. "My name is Trish," I said.

"Take the drink Trish, it'll be okay, I promise," Matt said before he left. There was an earnest look in his eyes and I was inclined to trust him. He didn't seem to hold my earlier actions against me and he was still the only one who had been open and honest with me from the beginning, the only one who had actually expressed concern for me. I offered him a smile and then he tore himself away.

Buck grinned, but it was without humor and his eyes were narrowed. He was the one I'd had the least interaction with, and I wasn't too upset about that. While Jack seemed strange and elusive, rough and intriguing, and Matt was kind and compassionate, Buck was just strong and powerful. There was no measure of mercy he wanted to give anyone and he hadn't expressed anything other than disdain for me. He shut the door behind him and stared at me.

"What do you want?" I asked.

"Nothing much. Just making sure that you're not going to try anything stupid again," he growled. His voice was low, rumbling like thunder.

"It almost worked. It would have worked, if I had known you were wolves and you could track me easily," I pouted.

Buck grinned. "I don't think so. You had no idea where you were going. If the Hunters hadn't found you, then another animal would have. There are dangerous creatures out there. It's not a place meant for someone like you."

"Like me? What do you mean by that? A woman?"

"A human," he said pointedly. I hushed after that and brushed the hair away from my face with a flick of the wrist. I folded my arms across my chest and regarded him coolly.

"And what would you suggest I do? Do you think I should just meekly accept what is happening? That doesn't seem likely if I have the blood of the wolf inside me, does it? Frankly I don't know what you want from me. If my bloodline is as strong as you say then surely you'd expect me to exhibit some strong characteristics, but you seem to just want me to hide away and accept everything that you tell me."

"Jack does," Buck shrugged. "He wants to protect you, and I'm pretty sure you can see why, where the Hunters are concerned. We got lucky that we took them by surprise today. But now they know for sure you're here they're likely to try again. We have to be prepared for them to try and take you. That's why I'm here, to make sure that nobody gets to you. And yes, if I were you I'd believe what we're telling you because we know more about this than you. You're clueless."

His words stung, mostly because they were accurate.

"Well that's not what Jack thinks," I said haughtily.

"No, well, Jack has his own ideas about things. I'm just doing what I can to hold the pack together. Time will tell if he's right about you." Something about the way he said it made my skin crawl.

"And what if he's not? Will I be allowed to go back to my old life?"

"That's for Jack to decide," Buck said. I can't say I was encouraged by his response. I pursed my lips as my gaze fell onto the cup Matt had left behind.

"Have you ever tried that?" I asked. Buck arched an eyebrow.

"It's a waste of time. I've said everything I want to say to people, and they've done the same for me. There's no sense in looking back, only looking forward. That's where Jack has gone wrong," he snarled. I got the impression that by leading him down this path I could get him to say more than he intended. I kept my voice low and calm so that I wouldn't alert him to the fact I was trying to tease information out of him. Buck was a strong man and wore his emotions on his sleeve, but he clearly didn't have the best idea of what he should and should not tell me.

"What do you mean?"

"Jack got this whole idea by speaking with his father. He wants to make the pack what it once was, strong and powerful with a lot of members. He wants to bring some glory days back and make this place a community again. But sometimes you can't fight the tide of the world. This was always going to happen. I'm just amazed that it took this long. The Wolves have always been an endangered species, ever since the beginning. We can't change the way nature works, we can only try to do the best with what we've got. Jack is fighting a losing battle, not that he listens to me. You can try it, if you want. It might make you see sense. I wouldn't know either way."

"I see. Well, it's nice to know you're so loyal to him."

"I'm not loyal to him. I'm loyal to the pack. It's the only thing that matters. Jack is the leader. That is his place. Unless he endangers the safety of the pack I shall obey his wishes. It could turn out that he's right." Buck walked to the table and peered at the liquid. "Maybe if you take this you might get a better idea of what's happening too. After all, I am just the muscle."

I wasn't sure about that. Buck seemed much more than that, but I wasn't going to try and get inside his mind. Instead, there was something else I wondered, although I didn't know if Buck was the right person to ask.

"What's it like, to be a wolf?"

Buck frowned. "It's better than you'll ever know. Now it's time for you to get back to your room. You've been out here long enough and I don't want to babysit you the whole time," he said, and opened the door. I didn't move. Buck came over and grabbed me by the arm, dragging me out. He brought the glass with him and handed it to me as he placed me back in the room. He slammed the door and locked it from the outside. I was imprisoned once again. My attempt to escape had been futile, but at least I now knew why they wanted me, even if I couldn't quite wrap my head around it.

I sat on the bed and drew my legs into my chest as I rocked back and forth, trying to decide if any of this actually made sense, or if I had lost my mind and this was all conjured by my psyche to distract me from the horror of my captivity. The three wolves had saved me, but did they actually care about me or did they just want me for what I could give them? They had great respect for my father, but aside from Matt they only really saw me as an object to be used, not a person with my own desires. I had to get through to them somehow and I had to gain a better understanding of what this all meant.

The only way to do that seemed to be through the Styx that Matt had given me.

The idea of taking this drug to transform my mind was frightening, but if it was the only way to gain some clarity then I saw no choice. As strange as it seemed, I was terrified that it might actually work and I could meet my father. I had spent my entire life waiting for this opportunity and now it had been given to me in the most unexpected circumstance.

Chapter Nine

My hands trembled as I reached out to the glass. I wasn't sure what awaited me, or if it would even work. Part of me thought it impossible, but then, hadn't I seen the impossible already? I had been thrust into a strange world where things weren't as they seemed and where miracles happened. If werewolves existed then there were no limits on what else could be true. My mind was a wreck, as I found the prospect of believing in all these things daunting. I would have much rather continued living in ignorance. I didn't know what the ramifications were for all of this, and now my idea of escaping and living off the glory of my story did not seem feasible. Who would believe any of this had happened to me?

I barely believed it myself.

But if I accepted that werewolves were true – and I pretty much had to, considering I had seen it happen with my own eyes; as much as I tried to explain it away as a hallucination or a drug there was no solution that made as much sense as the obvious truth – then why couldn't this drug be true too? I didn't think that Matt would lie to me; he had no reason to and no benefit to gain, unless this drug did something else and he wanted me to take it under false pretenses. It may well have been poison and they started to believe that I was more trouble than I was worth, but if they wanted to get rid of me there were easier ways. They could have just torn me apart with their claws. And if it was poison then, so what? I wouldn't have to live with this situation any longer. I wouldn't have to go through any more pain.

And I might actually get a connection with my parents.

That was the real truth of the matter. It filled me with fear and anticipation in equal measure. What would I even say to my father if I had the opportunity? I'd always imagined the conversation before; me in tears demanding an explanation of what happened, him protesting innocence, blaming it on Mom, before we finally found some common ground. Up until now it had always been a distant dream, a vague fantasy that likely wouldn't happen. It was one of those things that was easier to think about when the chances of it happening were slim. But it was an opportunity that I couldn't refuse.

I clasped the glass and brought it to my face. The midnight liquid swirled. I breathed in its scent, but to my surprise it was odorless. I closed my eyes as I brought the glass to my lips and gulped the liquid down. It was thick and viscous as it slithered down my throat. For a few moments afterwards nothing happened, but then the world around me began to shimmer. I dropped the glass and heard it shatter, but it was as though it happened far away. The shadows in the room became larger, looming figures that guarded the realm beyond the physical and the intangible. The sunlight that poured in through the narrow window dwindled until it was just a distant star in the sky, and then it winked out completely.

*

I was in a strange land, a land of shadow and mist and mystery. It was dark and shrouded, but I could see. The air around me shimmered with dark clouds that churned and, as I looked into the distance, black fog stretched out. As these clouds moved and danced around, there came an opening, and through this I saw the moon. It sparkled for an instant and then seemed to stretch out, coming at me through the aperture. The ground around me glowed and a wolf appeared. Its fur was the whitest white and its eyes were radiant gold. Fear struck me, but that feeling dissipated instantly as the wolf nudged my hand and started to walk past me, asking me to follow it. A tranquil feeling came over me and I followed its path.

The ground was hard like stone, but there was a layer of liquid above it that reflected all the churning morass of the fog around me. The world seemed to be without end. I was filled with the distinct feeling that I shouldn't be there. My flesh looked paler than usual. It was cast in a deathly pallor. This was a place that the sun did not touch. There was no plant life and no animals, apart from the wolf. It was devoid of anything other than the fog.

I can't say for certain how long I walked behind the wolf. There was no sense of the passage of time and the scenery didn't change around me so we might as well have been walking on the spot for all I knew. The wolf never looked back at me, just kept plodding forward, leaving footsteps upon the watery surface that disappeared as soon as he lifted his foot.

Eventually we came to a point where we stopped. The wolf tilted his head to the side and looked up. It howled, the purest howl there had ever been. The noise rose through the air and filled this world. It was deep and alluring, and I never thought I would describe a wolf's howl in that manner, but it was true. It was a thing of beauty and as the sonorous sound spread around me I believed in what Jack had been saying about magic. The wolf's song struck a chord in my heart and I was at peace.

As I marveled at the way the wolf inhabited this world, my gaze shifted to the swirling fog, which seemed to be shifting into a different form. I remembered why I had come on this quest and thought of Mom. The fog shifted and morphed and then a part of it came forward, separating itself from the mass. It took on a new shape and just as the men had shifted from wolves into men, this abstract fog shaped itself into a human, into the form of my mother. It wasn't quite perfect; the form moved oddly and there was only the barest hint of her expression, but there was no doubting that it was my mother.

Tremors erupted from my heart and I almost fell to my knees as she came to me.

"Mom I...how do you feel?" my words came out in a choking breath. I saw the mist shift and I could see her face. She smiled at me.

"I feel fine Trish. I feel wonderful and at peace."

I looked around and furrowed my brow in confusion. "In this place?" I asked.

Mom, or at least the form that looked like Mom, threw her head back and laughed. A shadowy hand crossed her chest to rest against her heart, the same way Mom always laughed. "It appears different to you than it does to me. The living are not supposed to be here, but there is so much to be discovered, so much more than I ever thought! You will learn one day Trish, and you will understand just as I have come to understand. Oh Trish, it is so good to see you."

Mom reached out. Tendrils of smoke caressed my cheek. The touch was cold and yet it was still imbued with affection.

"I sang for you," I said. My voice trembled. I tried so hard to maintain my composure, but it was just impossible. Emotion crept into my voice and tears welled up in my eyes.

"I know. I heard. It was beautiful," she said.

"Mom...what's going on? What's happening to me? Did you know about Dad?"

Her head tilted to the side in a very human way, which seemed odd coming from this shifting mass of clouds. The expression left her face in a moment of conflict, before it returned.

"I knew that something was different about him. I suppose that's one of the things that attracted me to him in the first place. As soon as we met I knew that I loved him. He was the only man that ever managed to fully capture my heart. The way he spoke...it was as though he knew that certain things were always going to happen. I couldn't resist falling in love with him. The time we spent together was short, but it left an indelible mark on my soul. I knew I would never be the same again. He was...he was so special to me and he told me that one day our child would be special as well, that he or she would go on to great things. I suppose that's why I pushed you so hard. I could only imagine one way in which you could be special. I'm sorry Trish. I shouldn't have been so narrow-minded about things."

"It's okay Mom. I know that you were just trying to give me the best life you could imagine for me. I'm sorry for being ungrateful and not seeing things from your point of view more. I wish that I could go back now and tell you all of these things, to make up for the time we lost."

"It's okay little one, we had a good life and you're telling me now."

I sniffed and wiped a tear away from my eyes, although more came afterwards, leaving my skin glistening in the pale light. "What happened with him Mom?" I asked. "Did he ever tell you anything about all this?"

"No...not in so many words. As I said he was different and I got the impression that he looked at the world in a different way. One day he disappeared. He had been worried about something for a while, although he wouldn't tell me what it was. Then I couldn't get a hold of him. I tried, but I assumed that like so many other men all his promises had been empty and once he'd gotten what he wanted he left."

"Why did you tell me he was an actor?"

"I didn't want you to go looking for him, or if you did go looking for him I didn't want you to find him. I wanted to spare you from that pain."

"He didn't leave you Mom. He was killed by these people called the Hunters, and he was different. He was...I don't even know how to say it."

"It's okay," Mom said in a reassuring tone, "I have a window into your soul Trish. I can also sense your conflict."

"I just don't know what to do. They kidnapped me and now they expect me to mother a new generation. But how can I give myself to them? How can I do this? I feel so lost and alone. I wish you were here to help."

"I am always with you Trish, always," she pointed to my heart. "You must look inside yourself and ask yourself what it is that you truly want. The world is a strange place and none of us knows our true place until we find it. I used to think that I belonged on a stage with thousands of adoring fans worshiping me, but that wasn't what I was meant for at all. I was meant to be a mother, to be your mother. There was always so much anguish in your life Trish, so much doubt about your place in the world. I can only tell you what it felt like when I was with your father. It felt right. It felt as though I belonged. Perhaps when you gain a proper understanding of things, you might realize the same. I don't know. But give these men a chance. They're scared for their pack and they're looking to you to be a mother. It is a great honor and a privilege. This aspect of the world...do you realize how few people get to see it? You have been blessed with knowledge," she laughed softly, "some might say it was a curse. But all I'll tell you is this; when you die you want to know that you have made a difference in life, that you have accomplished something. I was at peace when I died because I knew that no matter all the sins I had committed in the world, I had given you to it. You have been my salvation Trish and you will always choose the right path. You knew before I did that you weren't meant to be on the stage. You were meant for something greater."

Her head dipped and she caressed the side of my face again, before she drew her hands away. "I must go now. You have limited time here and there is another who wishes to speak to you."

Mom receded. The mist was pulled back, drawn into the larger undulating mass of the fog. I cried out, wanting her to stay. I reached out and tried to grasp her hand, but it was only air and it spread away from my fingertips as I tried to clasp her.

"Mom..." I cried in a cracked voice. Pain flared in my heart at having to say goodbye again, at having her taken from me again. "Why...why couldn't she stay?" I snapped at the wolf, but my words were weak and it offered nothing but a mysterious gaze in reply.

*

The wolf turned its head back towards the fog. Another form emerged, this one bigger and taller than Mom's. I recognized it instantly as the man from the picture. Jake. My father. I reeled back in horror, not entirely sure how to react or respond. He walked up to me and studied me. The shadows of his eyes were deep pits, and yet somehow they managed to express all kinds of emotion, mostly regret and sorrow.

"Daughter..." he said. "I'm sorry for what happened. I'm sorry for not being there to watch you grow and offer you guidance. I have...I have been watching and I've seen the pain. There are so many times I've wanted to reach down and help, but I have been unable to do so."

"Dad..." I said, so much emotion contained within that one small word.

"I know there is much you do not understand. I wish I could help you learn everything, but that is a journey you must take by yourself. What I can tell you is that Jack is a good man in his heart, he simply hurts and pain rules him at the moment. He can sense that the pack is dying. I sensed that same thing a long time ago... I wish I could have done more to help them."

"I saw the photos. The year after you died they were all so sad. You meant a lot to them."

"And they meant a lot to me. The same connection can happen with you as well, if you let it. I know they have not made the right decisions so far, but they mean well and they have done everything for the greater good. They care about the pack and they want to see it grow strong again. They want to protect innocents. These Hunters...they only want destruction and chaos. They want to spread pain and terror. The Howlers are the only thing standing in their way. Please Trish, I know that I wasn't there to help you grow up or to teach you anything. I wish I had because I would have taught you all about this world. I would have given you everything you needed to understand...but that opportunity was taken from me because of the Hunters. They took me from you, and they'll tear the pack apart if they have the opportunity."

"Dad I...it's so much. I don't know if I can do it. There's so much I don't understand."

"Look to the others. Use their strength. You can trust them. They won't hurt you. I promise. You are my daughter and you were meant for this. This is your legacy, your heritage. It is a lot to place upon your shoulders, but I know that you can carry the weight because you are my daughter. Your blood is strong, and from blood flows life. Cast all doubt from your mind and think about what this will mean to others. I know there has been much pain and conflict in your soul about your place in the world. Always you have been searching for where you belong. This is your place Trish. It may not be what you envisioned, but it is your destiny. You must carry on the work I started. You must protect the pack. Please...for me. You and the pack are the only things I left the world. Now you must go. Your time is short."

"No...Dad...wait! There's so much I don't understand. So much I want to talk to you about. There's just...so much. Dad. Please don't go! Not again!" I cried.

"I'm sorry Trish. I wish we had more chance to speak. One day we will. One day we will be reunited properly and we will make up for lost time. But until then you must remember that you are my daughter and that you are the one who can save the pack."

His words reverberated in my mind and my soul, as deep as thunder and as meaningful as prophetic words that had been spoken thousands of years before. Once again I was rendered an emotional wreck as his form returned to the fog, drifting far away from me. I had barely had any time with him, certainly not enough to make up for a lifetime of pain, but I had the feeling that all the time in the world wouldn't have been enough. Tears flowed down my cheeks as I looked at his receding form and I could see similar pain reflected in his shrouded expression. I saw his form stand by my mother's. They linked hands and for a moment I saw them together, finally reunited after he had been so cruelly taken from her, and to see them happy like that was to see a glimpse of the life that had been denied to me. I could have had a mother and a father who loved each other rather than just a mother who was jaded by heartbreak and overwhelmed by the needs of a child.

My heart burned with hatred for the Hunters.

My parents returned to the mist and as much as I wanted to stay with them I knew that it was time for me to return to the mortal world. I looked down at the wolf, and the wolf was looking back at me. It opened its jaws and howled once again, the sweet song filling my mind and my soul. The song expanded and reached into the farthest depths of this eternal world. The fog dissipated and cleared. The silver light of the moon spread and filled my vision with radiant light. Even the wolf seemed to get bigger, and I realized that I was sinking into the watery surface, a surface that had been as hard as stone underneath the liquid. It pulled me down. As my natural instincts kicked in I struggled and writhed to break free, but there was nothing to do but surrender. The liquid filled my mouth and swept over my head, the last thing to be submerged were my fingers as I sank back to reality. I was dark and cold, and filled with longing.

Chapter Ten

I awoke with a gasp of breath. My head pounded and I rubbed my temples to try and calm the raging pain. I had collapsed to the floor. The glass had shattered as I dropped it and shards of glass surrounded me. My eyes were bleary and my heart ached. There was some sense of closure given that I had spoken to my parents, but I still yearned to speak to them more. I rubbed my lips and a black smear smudged my thumb, a leftover from what I had drunk. Now that I was sitting in my cell again it was difficult to believe the journey I had taken, but I knew in my heart that it was real. Those were my parents and that place had been a bridge between the two worlds. I had a better sense of understanding of what I needed to do now and what my place in the world was. I was ready to accept my fate but I had to speak to Jack first.

I threw myself up and hammered at the door, pummeling it with my fists and yelling at the top of my lungs. I screamed and screamed until I heard footsteps approach from the other side and the lock turned. The door opened and Buck was standing there, looking down at me with a snarl.

"What do you want? It's better if you just keep quiet," he growled.

"I need to see Jack," I said.

"Buck, get out of the way!" Matt said, pushing past the big man. He came into the room and pressed his hands against my head, looking into my eyes. "Are you okay Trish? How are you feeling?"

I nodded as he released me. "I'm okay. I took the drink. I saw...I saw them Matt. It worked. Can you...can you make it so that I can see them again?"

"I'm sorry Trish, but as I said the root is rare. I used it all up to make that potion. I don't know when I'll find any again," he said. I nodded numbly, somehow knowing that was the case. I had broken the immutable laws of the world and I had to be satisfied with the one time of doing so.

"She looks okay," Matt said to Buck, "I don't think we'll be having any problem with her now," he said. He turned to me. I nodded. I didn't have any plans to escape. Where would I go and what would I do? I saw now that my life was largely meaningless without these wolves. I had always been meant to be a part of the pack. It was my destiny, as my father had always meant it to be.

*

It took some convincing from Matt but, eventually, he made Buck relent and escorted me through the clubhouse to Jack's room.

"It's going to be okay now, you'll see," Matt said, offering me a reassuring smile as he opened the door to Jack's room and showed me in, leaving me alone with the leader of the pack.

"So you had your journey to the bridge between the two worlds?" Jack asked. He was standing in the corner of the room with his back to me. His room was devoid of the personal touch. There was a bed, some clothes in a closet, and tattered books on a shelf. The window looked out on the meadow. Tools hung on the wall and he was fiddling with one of them when he turned to face me.

"Yes. Have you been on one?"

"A long time ago now," he said, betraying nothing with the tone of his voice.

"What do you call that place?"

"There are many different names. I like to call it the garden of the moon. Sometimes I wish I could visit it more often, but there is time for that in the future. There is still much to do here first."

"You mean the Hunters," I said. At the mention of their name his gaze flicked up and for a moment his blue eyes flashed gold. His lip curled and shadows fell upon his face.

"Yes, the Hunters," he said.

"My father mentioned them when I saw him," I moved into the room. "They seem to have been a problem for some time now. What exactly is their story?"

Jack moved away from the wall and sank on the edge of his bed. I remained standing. "All through our history there have been wars between packs of wolves. It is the nature of things to ensure that only the strongest pack survives. It's probably one of the reasons why we have had to live in the shadows. If we learned to work together we might have become even stronger, but that is not our way. Then the world started to change and people saw opportunities elsewhere. They started to leave this life behind and forge their own paths. The Hunters saw this and despised them for it. They believe that we should be eradicated, that any weakness should be culled. Sadly some members of our pack have joined theirs over the years. They believe that we should be wiped out and that they should be the only wolves left. They've always been brash and sought violent ends to things. So far we've managed to stave them off, but I fear that a great battle is coming, one that will define the future of wolves, and perhaps the future of the world."

"What do you mean?"

When Jack looked up at me I could see the emotion held within his eyes. "They won't stop with us. They see themselves as stronger than us and stronger than humans. To them it is a crime that they are not the dominant species and it is us weak wolves who have been holding them back. They wish to multiply and spread throughout the world, to declare war on humans and take territory for themselves. Their ambition matches their ruthlessness and I'm afraid to say that they will not relent unless they are stopped."

"Then you must stop them. They killed my father."

"I want to, but I cannot be sure which way the battle will go. First I must secure the bloodline. I must ensure that the pack will continue. That is the most important thing."

"My father said the same thing..."

"He was a wise man. Perhaps the best of us there has ever been." There was sheer reverence in Jack's voice. But there was a nagging doubt in the back of my mind, a gnawing thought that I just couldn't shake.

"What actually happened to him Jack? How did the Hunters get him? If he was so strong then how could he let this happen?" My voice trembled with worry. I hadn't been able to ask Jake how he died when I had been in the garden of the moon, but I had been curious.

"He didn't seek it out. There was a meeting and he was escorting women and children. The Hunters had been growing more threatening and the pack needed to know how to defend themselves and cope with the new threat. But there were enemies from within. They attacked and Jake was the only thing standing between the rest of the pack and death. He held the Hunters off while the rest of the pack escaped. There must have been ten of them at least, maybe more, and Jake lasted far longer than he had a right to. By the time help came he had massacred most of them, but the damage had been done. As soon as he knew the pack was safe he bled out and died. His sacrifice ensured that we would continue and thrive. The rest of the Hunters were hunted, and fought and defeated. Back then there were still enough of us to have superiority, but some of them escaped and have spent all this time rebuilding their pack, while ours has grown weaker and smaller."

I was proud of my father for being a hero and for giving his life to save the pack, but it didn't do anything to dispel my hatred of the Hunters. Because of them I had been denied a father. However, it did make me wonder if those same instincts were housed within my soul. I was his daughter after all, could I be that strong and that heroic when faced with danger?

Perhaps I would find out sooner than I would have liked.

"If you knew they were such a problem why haven't you done more to grow the pack?" I asked.

"I did," Jack's head hung down. "I had a mate."

"Oh," a flare of jealousy spiked in my soul. I wasn't quite sure where it had come from or what had inspired it. It shocked me, but I didn't explore it at this moment. "What happened?"

"What do you think happened?" Jack snarled. "Once the Hunters realized what was happening they got to her. They killed her. So now you understand why I wanted to keep you here for your own protection. I couldn't let the Hunters get near you. As soon as I saw you I knew that I had to bring you back here and keep you safe, that you were the one we had been waiting for, the one that could save us."

I moved closer towards him. I sensed the pain that was in his voice, and the pressure that weighed on his shoulders. He wanted to be the savior, he didn't want to be the last wolf in the chain, and for that he needed me. I suddenly realized what must have gone through his head that night when he saw me, how he must have caught a glimpse of hope and have the world open up to him, and how he was filled with the need to have me, no matter what. There was something about the instinctual, unpredictable, emotional need that flattered me more than if it had been a planned scheme. In me he had seen the one who could save his pack and he hadn't been able to resist taking me.

"Do you really mean that?" I asked. Nobody had ever spoken about me in this way, or felt this strongly about me. I wondered if it was the same kind of feeling that had so enraptured my parents when they had met. Jack licked his lips and clenched his jaw, but his gaze was still focused on the ground. His hands were clasped in between his legs.

"I do," he said simply. But I still had reservations in my heart. There was still one dream that I had wanted ever since I was little, and that was to fall in love and have the kind of life that had been denied to Mom. I could tell that she was lonely and now I understood why. At least she finally had her happy ending in the garden of the moon, but I wanted mine as well.

"Jack...I appreciate everything you're saying and what this pack means, not only to you, but to wolf society in general. But I also have to think of myself. And you have to start thinking of me as a person as well. I can't just be a tool for you to use to breed a new generation of wolves. I'm not some vessel that you can pass around your pack. Surely you must understand that I'd never agree to that, and if you want to subject me to that kind of treatment then surely you're no better than the Hunters? Do you really think my father would want you to treat me that way?"

Jack's head tilted up and he stared at me directly. "You don't understand, do you? I would never ask you to do anything like that," he rose from his bed and closed the distance between us. The air suddenly grew warm around me and breath caught in my throat. "After I lost Lucy I was certain that I'd never feel anything like real love again. She was my world, and if it hadn't been for the pack I would have died myself. But then I saw you and I heard your song and something changed. I tried to tell you outside, when we stood under the moon. There is magic in your voice Trish, magic that has healed the wounds in my heart. I know you may not believe me, but that moment was the first moment I fell in love with you."

"In love? Jack I...that's not possible. You don't even know me..." I said, taken aback by the force of his words. I staggered back, but he stepped forward and he placed a hand on my cheek. His flesh was warm and there was an intensity in his eyes that careened through my body. My heart pounded.

"Isn't it? Haven't you learned by now that anything is possible? I knew all I needed to know from that first song Trish. It spoke to my heart and I realized that you were the one we had been looking for, the one that could save us. I know all I need to know Trish. I'm a wolf. Our senses go beyond the physical world.

"But I don't know Jack. I'm not a wolf."

"You are. You may not be able to change into one, but you are a wolf in spirit, in your heart, and if you need more convincing then let me show you." Before I could say anything, he had pressed his lips against mine in a fervent, burning kiss. The passion scorched my lips and a soft whimper flowed out of my mouth. He gripped me tightly, preventing me from melting to the floor, and my skin began to tingle with so much passion I could barely comprehend it. His breath was hot and sweet, his tongue ardent, and his arms wrapped around me, completely enveloping me in his masculine warmth.

At first I was hesitant to kiss him back, but the intensity weakened my resolve and the pleasure that rose within me was intoxicating. If there was magic in my song then there was definitely magic in his kiss. His grip tightened upon my arms and I winced, pulling back as he pressed against the sensitive, bruised parts of my skin. Our breaths tore apart at the same time as our bodies.

"You're hurting me," I gasped. Shame flickered across his face as he looked at my arms and saw the small bruises that had been left by his fingers.

"I didn't mean..." he whispered, but couldn't bring himself to finish his sentence. He lifted my arm up and pressed his lips softly against my wounded skin. Pain blurred with pleasure as he kissed my bruised flesh. "Is that better?" he asked.

I smiled, and desire filled my eyes. "It's not the only part of me that hurts," I said. My body had been through hell and it still bore the wounds of my sprint through the forest. I showed him the wounds on my legs and stomach. He kissed up and down my shapely thighs, wrapping his hands around them like vines. He lifted my top up and kissed my stomach. My head tilted back and my lips parted slightly as a rush of breath flowed out of me. I knew it was wrong, that it was too soon, but I couldn't ignore the feelings inside. As he rose up he lifted the top over my head and I drowned in a kiss again, surrendering to the heat that engulfed me like an inferno. His hands were all over me and the way he kissed me...it was with the passion of a thousand raging suns.

His hands pressed into the small of my back. I could feel every sinew in his body tighten with desire. His breath was like fire and his kiss scorched me. My head grew hazy and light as these intoxicating, overwhelming feelings surged within, uncontrollably and relentlessly. My arms wrapped around his strong neck and I draped myself over him, for it was the only thing I could do lest I melt into a puddle on the floor. Oh what he had rendered me as...a helpless and desperate little thing. There was some silent spell he had cast upon me. It was the only explanation! How could I give myself to this man...this monster?

No, he wasn't a monster. He was a beautiful creature. I knew it was wrong. It didn't make sense in my mind, but I couldn't help the excitement that surged within me. We were both outcasts. Neither of us fit into the normal world, a world of careers and families and stable homes with mortgage payments and TV dinners. No, ours was a darker world, born of ancient dreams and hidden mystery. I was just a part of it, as he was and in a way it became clear to me that he, Buck, and Matt hadn't kidnapped me from my life; they had rescued me from it. I had been kidnapped a long time ago, forced into exile from the life that I was always meant to lead. My father had been taken from me by the Hunters. If he had still been around, the life I had led would have been far different...but I wasn't thinking about that at the time of course. I wasn't thinking about anything. My mind had been torn from my body, leaving nothing but pure thought and sensations.

I could taste the sweetness in the air and feel the heat that simmered from our bodies. I dragged my hand down his back as we collapsed onto the bed. It creaked under our weight and we soon became a writhing mass of flesh as we scrambled under the blankets, clawing at the rest of our clothes, seeking to free ourselves from the prison of our modesty. Jack was spurred on by primal energy. He bit and growled as he tore at my clothes and my flesh, squeezing tightly. He was going to leave bruises again, but this time I didn't mind. In fact I welcomed it. I groaned and my body arched as he bit my lip so hard he almost drew blood. I dug my nails into his flesh and felt the tremors through all the hard angles of his body. I felt his arousal pressing into me and my mind grew hazy with desire. All I wanted was to plunge myself into the darkness and lose myself in this abyss of pleasure.

I ran my hands through his hair as we kissed madly. Our tongues danced and our breaths barely escaped the cracks between our lips. Sweat prickled upon my skin. It became flushed, as rampant passion flooded my body. He took hold of my hands and pulled them above my head, pinning me down as he pressed into me. I felt the full weight of his body, and he felt glorious. My soft curves felt made to accommodate him. I melted into him and could feel myself becoming a part of him. His hands ran down my throat, over the rise of my breasts. I gasped as his palm brushed my hard nipple and tingles spread across my skin like a rippling wave. My mouth was agape and through my blurred vision I could see him smirk. For a moment I felt entirely vulnerable, and I couldn't believe what he had reduced me to. Never before had anyone reduced me to such a whimpering mess or caused such chaotic desires to crash through me. I had never been seized by this delirious exhilaration and the madness swept through me with such fervent desire that I couldn't comprehend just how he was tearing me apart inside!

The magic of his hands moved down my body, over my flat stomach, finding my burning inner thigh. He squeezed. I whimpered. Even just a gentle caress of his hand was enough to begin a cascading tidal wave within me. The magnitude of it was such that I wanted to fight it. There was a tight knot in the middle of my body. I trembled as I tried to force my legs closed, tried to stop the damp wetness that throbbed, all because I was afraid of the intensity of the pleasure. But what use was my fear against his desire. He had set his sights on me from the very beginning, had marked me as his because of my song and now he was claiming me properly. Quaking desire danced across my skin and his hands forced my legs apart. My head arched back and my lips parted as a guttural moan escaped my throat. My eyelids fluttered shut as his long, deft fingers found the heat and explored the molten core of my body. All at once I felt tense and relaxed, and burning energy radiated from my flesh. With one soft curl he was able to elicit deep and sensual feelings, reaching deeper inside me than anyone had ever reached before. It was as though he was an expert on my body from the start, knowing just how to make me writhe and how to find my secret sweet spots.

Excited sweat trickled down my face and in between the valley of my breasts, just as all my desire flowed out past his fingers and down my slick thighs. He whispered things in my ear, secret things, hot things, things that merged with my thoughts, creating incoherent, wonderful feelings inside me. My hands played with his flesh, feeling the paths of his muscles. I wanted to drown in him. His lips slipped over mine, silencing my moans as his fingers beckoned forth a shuddering, trembling orgasm that ran through me like a wave. I clutched onto him as I felt him inside me, making me dance like a puppet to his whims, this man, this wolf, this Jack.

I was breathless as he pulled away and kissed my neck. I raised a leg and felt the uncomfortable heat of my own desire slipping down in a torrent. My skin glistened, and I could not tear my eyes away from him. He was the epitome of a man. I ran my fingers down the thick bed of hair on his chest. For a moment I let my fingers linger against his heart, losing myself to the powerful thumping rhythm. I buried myself in the crook of his neck as my hands ran farther down, across his flat stomach, following the trail of a thin line of hair that snaked to forbidden dark areas. My fingers danced across the thick thatch of hair, drawn to his heat, and then I was with him. The taut skin burned my fingers as I curled my hand around. The rippling veins were filled with passion. I groaned as he was so tall and strong, so big and thick, and so hard for me... for me.

As I started to play with him he kissed me deeply and my hands found a natural rhythm. I followed the sounds of his moans and his ardent gasps as I teased him, squeezing hard before I dragged my nails up the underside of his shaft and then over the smooth, sensitive tip. He shuddered and I was flooded with pride as I knew that I was responsible for making him feel this way, that I was the one bringing the wolf to his knees.

I had thought everything had flowed out of me, but there was still more. It flared and bloomed inside as our bodies pressed together and I lost all sense of time and space. In that moment it didn't matter that I had been kidnapped. There was no other place in the world that I would rather have been. Our lips caught each other and I needed him inside me. Thought blurred with speech and I wasn't sure if we were communicating verbally or if somehow we just knew what each other were thinking. I transcended to a new realm, one of ethereal delight. Our bodies moved in harmony. He massaged my breasts and then leaned down to tease my nipples with his mouth and tongue. Hot breath washed over me, causing me to tense my grip on him, which made him grunt with bestial desire. For a moment I thought his eyes flashed gold, but I couldn't be sure. He pulled my hand away and pinned it beside me, kissing me deeply. I knew what was coming. I wanted it so badly. He reached down. Our bodies adjusted naturally, dancing the ancient dance that had been performed so many times before. There was a moment of uncertainty and anticipation before – yes – that sweet feeling of bliss as our bodies came together. My entire body arched and my eyes closed. I felt his head sink into me and a long exhalation drifted out of him and for a moment we were suspended in time, enjoying the eternity of this moment where we could be connected forever.

And then he started moving. I held onto him tightly as he reached deep inside me, stretching me to my limits. His hips rolled like a flowing tide and I took everything he had to give me. The warmth seared through me as though I had been filled with lava. I lay back and surrendered to all the fervent desires within me. They unspooled, as thick as honey and as intoxicating as the most powerful alcohol.

Pleasure surged within and my body shuddered with orgasmic ecstasy as so much was released. It was as though all this swirling, miasmic primal energy had been locked inside me for so long and was only now getting released. It had been building up to incomprehensible levels and now it burst out like a phoenix escaping the flames, crackling and scorching my body as it left and rose like an escaping phantom. A long, low growl escaped my lips but it was distant somehow, as though it had come from something other than myself and I realized that I had ascended from the trappings of my body to become a being of pure energy and sensation. I could feel the thread that bound all of us together, most specifically me and Jack. I was intimately attuned to all of his movements and his feelings too. I tasted the sweat that dripped off him and sizzled on my skin. I felt every undulating movement as his body crashed against mine. In that moment he was the entire world to me and I held on to him for dear life. The heat was almost unbearable, but I could not let go as I felt him getting harder and faster, and everything came in a torrent. I locked eyes with him and I was stunned by the force within his gaze. I realized then that he was a part of a most ancient line, and that I had a legacy as well. We were both children of the moon and as I was blessed by this revelation the final pleasure hit, the thunderous crash of his orgasm. I felt the trembling tension of his body rising within before it happened, and then it hit me like a lightning bolt as he released himself in a vibrant paroxysm that contained within it so many raw emotions.

I was left gasping and breathless as the sensations blazed through me and we stayed connected while the echoing aftermath reverberated through our bodies. Our foreheads pressed against each other as our panting breaths mingled and he kissed me again, this time more tender and delicate. My body throbbed and ached, delirious and drained after what I had shared with Jack, but a great many things made more sense now and I was beginning to see how I could fit into this world.

Jack rolled off me and lay on his back. I stared up at the ceiling, my chest heaving with every heavy breath. The heated feelings dissipated and left me with something raw. Once all the passion of the lovemaking had been taken away there was nothing but the cold, pure emotion. Often people had regrets in the aftermath of making love as the instinctive desire overrode all kinds of rationality. The union between Jack and I had been so sudden and unexpected that when it was over I worried I would be overwhelmed with regret, but even when reason entered my mind again I was only filled with satisfaction. Yes, it was unconventional, but I was drawn to Jack in a way that didn't feel wrong. Now that I knew my history I had a better grounding of who I was and what I wanted in the future. I had never fit in, in the outside world, my place was here, with Jack and the other wolves. I was beginning to accept it, how could I not when I had never felt at ease in the other world? Mom was right; I had always been meant for something more special than the real world. She thought it had been Hollywood but she was wrong; it had been this motorcycle club and these wolves.

Chapter Eleven

Our sweat soaked bodies glistened in the fading light. The windows in his room were bigger than the one in my cell. Silver light poured in and I couldn't quite believe that I had just slept with the leader of the pack. He had peeled away all my layers of defense and showed how hopelessly yearning I was for a connection with him. I wasn't sure at which moment I realized I wanted him, but the torrent of emotions had surged through the floodgates of my heart and I couldn't stop myself. Where he had been rough with me before, he had shown tenderness during our lovemaking. I nestled into him and draped my arm over his chest. Drops of sweat lingered on the curled ends of his chest hair. Under my palm I could feel his heart beating, powerful and frantic as he tried to compose himself after our heated session. His chest rose in deep breaths, as did mine. I kissed him softly and tasted the salty sweetness of his skin, murmuring as the lingering sensations flowed through my body.

I fit nicely into the crook of his arm and I could have stayed there for an eternity. I looked up, expecting to see desire playing upon his face, but there was a stony expression.

"What's wrong?" I asked, my voice barely a whisper.

"I'm thinking of the future and all that is yet to come."

"Try to put it out of your mind. No good is going to come of this," I said, but it evidently wasn't going to work. He pulled my arm off him and slid out of bed, moving to the window. The moonlight that poured in silhouetted his body, highlighting all the perfect angles of his muscles. I wrapped the blanket around me and sat up. My hair fell upon my shoulder in ringlets. My body still simmered with the passion he had conjured within, and my breaths were deep gulps.

"But I must think and plan. I know that the Hunters are out there, waiting to make their move. They see us as vulnerable and they know what having you here means for us. I will not let them take you from me. I will not let them harm you like before."

"With Lucy," I said in a hushed whisper. His head hung. "She meant a lot to you, didn't she?"

"She meant everything."

"Tell me about her."

"I...it would not be right."

"Please, Jack, I want to know," I said, longing to feel some of his deep emotion and to explore what feelings lay in his heart. From making love with him I could tell that he was a man who felt things deeply and whose roughness was a façade, shielding his sensitive soul from hurt and pain, holding it deep within until it seeped into his bones. "You should be able to share these things with me if I am to be the mother of your pack," I said.

He looked directly towards me.

"Do you mean to say that you have accepted your role, your duty?"

I considered the question for a moment. Emotions swirled within me. I knew there were so many things I hadn't yet thought of, and no doubt there would be other surprises in store, but after being intimate with Jack I knew that he wasn't going to treat me as an object and that this was something greater than merely being used as a vessel for the continuation of the pack. He cared for me, truly cared, and while I didn't know about the other men in the pack I was ready to trust him.

"Yes, I am. But what will people think about you and I being together?"

"They will accept it because I am their leader." He walked over and cupped my head in his hand, stroking my cheek with his thumb. "If I had my way I would not allow anyone else to touch you, but I must think of the pack," he said.

"Was it like that with Lucy?" I asked, determined to root into his past. He smirked and let out a small chuckle, evidently realizing that I was like a dog with a bone when it came to certain matters.

"No, it wasn't. She was my sweetheart. We grew up together and for all my life I thought we were going to end up living our lives together. She was kind and sweet. She valued the pack as much as I did and wanted to make it great again. She longed to have children and to fight back against the Hunters. I have never met anyone as pure in spirit as her, and it was such a tragedy that she was not given a chance to live her life the way she wanted. She was taken from us too early, just as your father was." He turned away from me as sorrow pervaded his heart.

I rose from the bed. The blanket slipped away, leaving me naked. I placed my hand on his shoulder and pressed my body against his. "Then we will avenge them both, Lucy and my father, and anyone else the Hunters have hurt. But Jack…you can't treat me like you have done before. You must let me make my own decisions. I know you wish to make this pack strong, but I will not sleep with anyone I do not wish to." I wanted to make that very clear from the beginning. Jack nodded, wrapped his arm around my waist and pulled me into him again for a passionate kiss. Fire swelled within my heart and I lost all sense of time and space as he dragged me to the bed. We fell upon the sheets and animal passion overwhelmed me again. The last thing I saw before I descended into darkness was mother moon smiling down on me, on us, blessing us with her silver stare.

*

I awoke with a smile on my face. A good ache rippled all through my body and a satisfied murmur purred between my lips. I enjoyed the warmth of the bed. It still radiated heat from our night together. I luxuriated in it as though it was a warm spring in a sunny glade, a place where I could cast away all the trappings of civilization and enjoy the natural desires of sun kissed skin in a crystal lake. I sighed happily, basking in this glory, but my mood quickly changed when I reached over to feel him, but grasped nothing but air.

I spread my palms over the imprint of his body. The bed was still warm. I pushed myself up. Confusion danced upon my face as I looked around the room and saw no sign of him. I didn't understand...it felt as though we had made a real connection and I couldn't see why he would leave without waking me or telling me. I told myself to not worry, that I was likely overreacting and becoming paranoid, but the night had been so wonderful and I had finally gained some equilibrium, I did not want to lose it or risk anything unbalancing it. There had been enough twists and turns for my liking. I just wanted it to be over and to find a steady foundation. So much of my life had been cast in the shadow of turmoil and I just wanted it to be over.

Pulling on my clothes, I flung the door open and walked out through the clubhouse. Things were eerily quiet and the short hairs on the back of my neck rose in alarm. I swallowed the lump of fear in my throat, but it wouldn't go away. Something was desperately wrong and I feared the worst. I checked all the rooms I had been in before, but there was no sign of anyone and none of the usual sounds either. The doors to the main hall waited for me, called to me, but I hesitated in fear as I was afraid of what I might find.

I turned the handle and peeked through the crack. The main bar was a large room with a pinball machine, TV, dart board, poker table, pool table, and lots of other tables and chairs scattered around. The bar was well-stocked and the smell of cigars, grease, and alcohol created a potent cocktail. As I glanced around I couldn't see anyone and I wondered if they had all left. It would have been ironic; the moment I was able to leave I had figured out that I wanted to stay. Why couldn't this have happened a couple of nights before?

But no...I was glad that it hadn't. If I had escaped and returned to my normal life I never would have discovered the truth about my father and I never would have gotten closure with my mother. It still amazed me that I had been on that journey. I intended to thank Matt properly the next time I saw him. I realized now that I had mistreated him for he had been genuinely kind to me. I had been wrong about all the wolves, aside from Buck. He was as mean as he looked and I wasn't disappointed at the thought of not seeing him again.

Then I opened the door a little wider and stepped into the room. As I entered I got a wider view of the bar and as I crept around past the bar I saw that by the main door to the clubhouse Buck was sitting with his legs up on a table, sipping from a beer.

"Well, good morning to you," he said, tipping the bottle towards me. I glowered and my cheeks turned red. My hands clenched into tight balls as I stormed up to him, annoyed that he was the one who had been left behind.

"Where is everyone? Where's Jack?" I frowned as I spoke. Buck moved slowly, swinging his legs down from the table and then rose from his chair. His biceps were on full display as the sleeves had been cut away from his denim vest. It struck me as vain, but his biceps were impressive and I couldn't help but admire them, despite my better intentions.

"That's no way to act after you've just gotten up. Go and get yourself a drink and something to eat. There's nothing to do but relax," Buck said casually. His eyes gleamed with amusement and he clearly took great joy in torturing me, which only made me more frustrated.

"Where's Jack?" I repeated, this time more tersely, through gritted teeth. Buck folded his arms and regarded me with a wry stare. His smile was slanted and he placed his beer down on the table.

"Jack has gone to speak with the Hunters," Buck said. The color drained from my face and my jaw dropped.

"He what?"

"He went to speak with the hunters. Last night a message came to us. Turns out that after our little scrap in the forest they want to talk and try to sort things out. I guess now that they've finally tasted blood they're willing to negotiate, or at least that's what they claim," Buck said. A hint of pride crept into his voice as he referred to the wolf he had killed. The image of that dead wolf filled my mind. At the time it had been easy to forget that it was a man. A shiver of fear crept down me as I realized that perhaps I was not as prepared to be a part of this world as I thought. There was a side of it that was vicious and deadly.

"You don't think that's true?"

"After all the crap they've pulled over the years? No way," Buck scoffed. He picked up the bottle and took a swig. "They aren't interested in peace. I tried telling Jack that, but he said we owed it to everyone to at least see if there was another way out of this. He seemed to think we might be able to get some information about their numbers as well. We haven't really been able to send out scouting parties for fear of losing men," Buck said.

"Where do they even live?"

"In the town that used to be the home of our community," Buck snarled. "But it's a trap. It has to be."

"I'm surprised you're not there with them. I would have thought they'd want their most powerful wolf," I said. I was trying to get under his skin, but it didn't work. He just wore that same slanted smile again, and I found it was me who was getting agitated.

"I thought the same thing, but there's enough of them going that they should be able to take care of themselves. Jack wanted me back here to defend you, in case this is all some elaborate plan to get to you. Matt's here as well, but he's out in the meadow gathering herbs in case a lot of healing is needed. So it's your lucky day, you're stuck with me," he sat back down and stretched his arms behind his head, pushing out another chair, gesturing for me to sit down. I looked at it and felt annoyed that Jack had deemed it fit to leave without even telling me. I refused to sit down and instead went to the bar. I pulled out a packet of chips and a bottle of beer. It wasn't the healthiest breakfast, but I needed something to quell the aching doubt in my gut.

When I muttered my displeasure about Jack's actions, I did so without thinking, and of course Buck responded.

"There's still a lot for you to learn Trish. When you get to know Jack better you'll start to realize that he's not the most reliable person. He's the leader of the pack and that matters to him above everything. He's going to do whatever he thinks best, no matter what, and there's no use talking him out of it, you just have to go with the flow."

"I see. Well I'm glad I have you and your words of wisdom here," I said bitterly. "But it's not as though you care about anything other than the pack either. You've already told me that you're only goal in life is to keep the pack together."

"Yeah, because I've seen how easily it can be torn apart," Buck said. For a moment the confident smirk disappeared from his face and he scowled. There was a darkness in his eyes that intrigued me and hinted at a deeper soul.

"What do you mean?"

"It doesn't matter. You don't need to know."

"Buck, come on, if we're going to be stuck in here together then you might as well tell me. It's not like we've got anything better to do. And you never know, talking about it might help," I said. Buck leaned forward and he looked as though he was about to speak when he suddenly twitched and his ears pricked up. He cursed under his breath and rose abruptly, grabbing me by the arm and dragging me out of the bar.

"What are you doing?!" I cried. "Get off me!" he opened the door and flung me inside. His eyes were intense.

"Stay out of sight. They're here," he said, and those words were enough to make my heart sink. Fear crawled all over me and I suddenly felt vulnerable again, as vulnerable as I had when the three men had first approached me outside of the bar. But they had turned out to have good intentions. I knew these Hunters didn't. Buck slammed the door behind me and returned to the bar. He was the only defense I had, and as a last line of defense went he was a pretty damned good one, but I had seen how deadly the Hunters could be and I didn't want to sit there helplessly and do nothing.

I pushed the door open and kept low as Buck opened the door. His enhanced senses had allowed him to hear the approaching Hunters far before I did, but the roar of their motorcycles soon became apparent and it only made my fear increase. Buck stood at the doorway, hands on his hips. His frame was a silhouette and he waited patiently for them to approach. Out of the wide windows I saw the three of them, each of them meaner looking than the last, all burly and stocky. They walked slowly and pulled off their gloves. Buck walked back inside while I scurried behind the bar, hiding in fear. There was a gap between the bar and a handily placed mirror, so I could see everything that went on.

The three Hunters approached the bar.

"Where is she?" one of them growled.

"I don't know what you're talking about. There's only me here. I guess that the peace talks haven't gone well?" Buck replied. He took a sip of his beer and didn't seem troubled at all. I couldn't help but be impressed by how cool he was under pressure, especially considering that he was outnumbered three to one. Even though I had seen how viciously he had fought in the forest I was still afraid for him, as I didn't think such a thing could be repeated, not without any backup. I thought about running to the meadow to try and find Matt but I didn't dare move now in case they saw me.

"Ha, peace was never on the table. Your leader is a fool if he believed that we'd ever consider making an agreement with you."

"It seems we have at least one thing in common then," Buck said. "But unfortunately for you it's just me here, and you really should have stayed at home." Buck took a final swig of his beer and then launched the bottle at the first man. In a rage he threw himself at the three men and pummeled them as hard as he could. He shoved tables to try and separate them and drove chairs into their chests. He moved in such a flurry that it was almost impossible to keep track of him. Everything was a weapon and for a moment I thought that my fears had been misplaced. He was so strong that it didn't seem anything could dare stand up to him. His long arms reached out in thrashing punches, he twisted and turned and seemed to know where the Hunters would be before they even moved. It was a raw, violent dance and I was captivated by it.

But then the Hunters started to fight back.

Chapter Twelve

I clamped my hand over my mouth, stifling my anxious gasps as the Hunters overcame the confusion borne from the initial flurry of Buck's attacks and regrouped. They fought as one and Buck wasn't being as successful at fending them off as he was before. When he jabbed at one, another came in and thrust a hook in his gut. He still took a lot of punishment and lasted much longer than any other man would have in the same situation, but it seemed as though there was only going to be one conclusion.

The hunters wrestled him down. A table crashed under the weight of the four men. Buck wriggled amid the maelstrom of arms and flesh, and managed to free himself with a mighty roar. He squirmed away and ran to the pool table where he grabbed a cue and started flailing it around wildly. The Hunters recoiled at first, but then one of them grabbed the end and Buck's attack stopped, at least with the cue. But he pulled the Hunter towards him and stuck out his arm. The Hunter's face crashed into Buck's forearm and there was a crunch as his nose broke. It must have been like running into a brick wall.

I stayed as quiet as I could. I knew the Hunters were wolves, and that their senses were enhanced just like Buck's had been. For the moment they seemed too focused on Buck for anything else to matter, but I knew that could change quickly. I hoped that the stench of alcohol and grease could at least mask my scent for a little while.

Buck snarled. His body bristled with primal energy.

"You killed Johnny the other day," one of the Hunters said. "I'm glad you're here. I can get revenge for him."

"You can try," Buck said, and then it happened. He'd finally had enough of fighting in a human form. The air shimmered around him and his face changed. Even as I watched I could barely believe it was happening. Grey fur sprouted from his flesh and the muscles became even more pronounced. His face lengthened into a snout, but the snarl was still there and the aggression was still contained within those beady eyes. He hunched over, his bare teeth ivory sharp, and as he transformed so did the Hunters. Their fur was black and patchy, they were stocky and leaner, looking in worse health. Saliva dripped from Buck's mouth as he growled and flung himself forward again. This time though, instead of throwing punches, there were snapping jaws nipping in every direction and swiping claws seeking to tear flesh from bones. The tables and chairs were obstacles in the arena that were flung asunder. Buck slammed into one of the Hunters with a raging ferocity and aimed to bite him in the neck, but at the last moment the Hunter adjusted his position and Buck sank his teeth into his shoulder. The Hunter yelped in pain, but it wasn't as deadly as it could have been.

The other two Hunters nipped at Buck's body, trying to take advantage of their numerical superiority. I felt helpless cowering behind the bar and knew that I had to do something. Once they got past Buck they would tear this place apart looking for me, and then I would follow. I winced as I heard the sickening sound of flesh being torn apart and the painful yelps. Buck was still managing to hold his own, but there was only so long that he could last. One of the Hunters butted his head into Buck's chest and sent him staggering back. His arms were askew and his chest was open. One precise attack and his body would have been slashed open. I was about to cry out in the hope that I might be able to distract them, but I was rendered silent by the Hunter's attack. The wolf with the darkest fur launched itself at Buck and for one terrible moment I thought it was all over. But then Buck shifted his position to the side and brought his paws down, catching the wolf and helping it on its way, straight through the window. It crashed outside and the window shattered in a thousand sprinkling shards of glass. The wolf landed with a thud and a whimper. The Hunters looked shocked and Buck took advantage, charging at one and sinking his paws into it, sending it flying across the bar.

The only problem was, Buck had been so lost in a rage that he wasn't thinking and the wolf was flung straight towards me. It landed on top of the bar and it scrambled up. I cowered, trying to hide myself, but the bar was my only cover. I hoped that the wolf had been so shaken by its ordeal that it would not notice me, but it was a forlorn hope. As soon as it laid its eyes on me its tongue lolled out of its mouth and it let cry a terrible howl, a howl that told its allies that they had found what they were looking for. The great pride of the Howlers: Me.

It regained its balance and swiped with a deadly paw. I felt the air rush by my face and fear rippled through me at the sight of the blood-stained claws. In a panic I grabbed anything I could find. My fingers curled around the neck of a heavy bottle and I smashed it over the wolf's head. The bottle smashed and I used the jagged edges to poke at the wolf. I didn't care where I aimed. I didn't even know if I had hurt it, but the wolf reared back and slid off the bar. I clutched the bottle close to me, and caught my reflection in the mirror as I stood up. I was as white as a sheet and my body shook violently. The wolf scrambled to its feet and snarled. Its lips trembled and it was about to make another attack when Buck leapt forward and dug his claws into the wolf's back. The wolf arched back and twisted his neck, trying to snap at Buck, but Buck's claws were too far away for it to connect. The wolf wriggled and writhed as it tried to get free, but the only way it could escape was to tear itself away, literally, leaving some of its fur and flesh behind on Buck's claws in a bloody mess. Buck pushed it away and went to pursue, but as he did the other wolf came rushing by in a dark blur. Buck twisted to try and stop it, but his flailing grasp grabbed only air.

There was nothing but the bar standing between the wolf and I.

It leapt and its paws found the surface of the bar, using it as a springboard to leap forward. I waved the bottle above me in a slashing arc, but as I opened my eyes the wolf was behind me. Its paws were on the ground and its eyes were locked onto me with an intense gaze.

Every sinew in its body was primed for death. I backed away, throwing bottles at it. They landed on the floor and smashed, making alcohol leak out onto the floor. It dripped off the wolf's paws as it came towards me. I held the bottle in both hands now, fear making them tremble so much I was afraid that I would drop the only weapon I had.

Then my back hit the bar.

There was nowhere else to go.

I dared not take my eyes off the wolf, but I twisted my head and my gaze flicked away for a moment, just a moment to see if Buck was there to come in to save me. My heart sank as I saw that he was locked in a battle with the other wolf. I could see him struggling to break free. The other wolf wasn't even trying to kill him, it was just trying to stop Buck from getting to me. Buck tore at the enemy but it was no use, and then looming behind him was the wolf he had thrown outside. It was back with a lust for vengeance in its heart, covered in blood, and the shards of glass that stuck in its fur sparkled as the sunlight caught them. It was almost beautiful, had it not been so horrific.

I turned back, my head moving slowly as the wolf's teeth dripped with death. I could almost feel them sinking into my flesh, releasing my soul from this mortal prison. I had wanted more time with my parents, but not like this. Never like this...

Breath choked out of me, helpless prayers to a god I didn't believe in, that I might be saved from this gruesome and grisly fate. The wolf was undeterred by anything I could throw at it. It might have flinched, its approach may have been delayed for a brief moment, but its path was as inexorable as destiny. Behind me I could hear Buck howling in anguish. I hoped for anything. I hoped for a miracle. I could feel the stale breath of the wolf drifting towards me, warm and fetid, hungry for my flesh. The sharp edges of the bottle didn't seem enough. It was wary, its eyes followed the path of the bottle, waiting for the opportunity to strike. I didn't know if I could move swiftly enough to defend myself, or even hurt it enough to dissuade it from attacking. Even if I struck it, it was likely going to do damage to me, more damage than I could do to it.

But then my miracle came.

Crashing through the doors came Matt. He was already in the form of a wolf and his tawny brown fur was a welcome sight. He was not the biggest wolf, but he was ferocious, especially when defending something he cared about. He leapt behind the wolf that was attacking me and sank his teeth into its back, subduing it. The wolf was in such close quarters that it could not maneuver properly and its slashes were aimless and helpless. Matt dug his teeth in relentlessly and used his claws to tear open the side of the wolf. Crimson gushed out and I almost gagged. It mixed with the alcohol in a grim pool.

Once Matt was done with that wolf he leapt past me and went to help Buck. I turned to see that Buck was still struggling with the two wolves, although he had endured for far longer than I had expected. The remaining two Hunters were snapping their jaws and slashing their claws at him. Buck's grey fur was stained with blood and patchy where they had attacked him. He looked groggy and his thrusting limbs weren't moving as freely as before, and I had a feeling that it was only due to the other wolves that he was still standing.

Matt streaked in with a howl and bit one of the Hunter's legs. He staggered and crumpled to the floor. It was the one who had already been tossed through the window and it seemed as though his body had suffered all the pain it could handle. The limbs twitched as he struggled to rise again, but neither his body nor soul was strong enough to hang on, and his head lolled to the side.

Without him attacking, Buck teetered on his feet and crashed, slamming against a table, breaking it in two. The last Hunter had lunged forward to attack Buck, but now that Buck was no longer there the Hunter was off balance. Matt took full advantage of this. He may not have been the strongest wolf, but he was wiry and wily, and his intelligence was just as much an asset as brute strength. He threw all his weight into his attack, sending the Hunter crashing to the floor, sprawled on its back with its limbs splayed out and its belly exposed. Matt brought both paws up and bared his claws, and then brought them down with the full force of his weight behind the blow. There was a sickening squelching as Matt fell upon the last Hunter, and then there was peace.

*

I sank to the ground, my watery knees finally giving way beneath me. When I realized that I was still clutching the broken bottle, I threw it down. I gazed up and saw the wolf's lifeless eyes staring at me. Its flesh had been torn and the blood was slowly creeping towards me. I shuddered and yelped as I pushed myself away just before it could reach my toes and ran back out in front of the bar, where I saw that Matt and Buck had returned to their human forms.

Matt was hunched over Buck.

"No...no," he gasped. I was filled with sorrow as well. Buck had done all he could to defend me. I owed him my life and whatever dislike of him I'd had before had completely disappeared. Sometimes you couldn't judge people on what they said or thought, only on what they did, and when it mattered, Buck had protected me. I rushed towards Matt's side and tears welled up in my eyes. Buck looked so weak. Now in his human form, it was easier to see the cuts and the slashes. Now that I could see the wounds properly I was even more amazed that he had managed to withstand the brutal attack of three Hunters. Blood trickled down the side of his mouth and gave his lips a scarlet glow, as though he had been wearing lipstick. His eyes fluttered, but there was no coherent thought behind it.

"I'm so sorry Matt," I groaned.

"Go out into the corridor. I have my satchel there. Grab it for me," he said, his words imbued with intensity. He didn't take his eyes or his hand off Buck, whose head he cradled. I nodded and rushed out, wiping the tears from my eyes as my vision was a blur. His satchel had been left by the doors and I hooked my arm around the strap, returning quickly through the double doors and handed it to Matt. He opened the pouch and rummaged through it, bringing out a few different kinds of flowers and herbs. The fragrant aroma was a welcome change from the smell of death and blood that rose all around us, but it was only a vivid burst.

"Go behind the bar and grab me some rum," Matt said. It was the most assertive he had ever been, and I have to admit I liked it. I went behind the bar again and tried to ignore the wolf that lay there. Irrational fear gripped my mind; I was so afraid to turn away in case it came to life again, but despite having been exposed to so many impossible things I knew that some things were just beyond any kind of reality.

I had to focus on the task at hand anyway, for Buck's sake. I couldn't let my swirling thoughts distract me from potentially saving him. To my horror though, I realized that most of the bottles I had thrown at the wolf had been rum.

"What if there is no rum?" I asked, my voice trembling.

"I need rum!" Matt cried.

I scowled as I redoubled my efforts and searched every nook and cranny of the bar. I eventually found a bottle in the shadows of a compartment, and brought it back to Matt.

He took it from me gladly and unscrewed the lid, pouring the rum into a glass. Then, he pinched the stem of a flower from his pouch and slipped his thumbnail down the middle, opening it up. Clear sap trickled out and he squeezed it into the glass. Then, he took a leafy herb and tore off a wide leaf, shredding it before he scattered it in the concoction. It had a light smell and as the aroma drifted to my nose it lifted my mind. Matt curled his hand around the glass and lifted it to his nose, breathing in the scent of the aroma. He swirled it and then took a sip, winced, arched his eyebrows and then nodded.

"Is that going to save him?" I asked.

"I hope so," he said. He gently lifted Buck's head and pressed the glass against his lips. The liquid slipped in and Matt had to tilt Buck's head from side to side to induce him to swallow the liquid. Some of it trickled out and spilled onto the floor, but most of it went inside. My chest tightened as I hoped dearly that Buck would be saved.

"We need to get him somewhere more comfortable. Do you think that you could help me carry him?" Matt asked. I looked at Buck's bulky body and then down at my own tiny frame and gulped.

"I can try," I answered. I was already feeling weak from the ordeal and had to force myself to stand. Neither Matt nor I were the strongest, but we struggled to get Buck up, trying to use whatever we could to help support us. We hooked our arms underneath Buck's body and it was like trying to tip a mattress, but in the end we managed to get Buck on his feet. His weight almost crushed me as I slung his arm around my shoulder and wrapped my other arm around his waist. Matt groaned too as we slowly moved him to the back, to his own room, where we placed him on the bed. We placed him there as softly as we could, but even so he landed with a thud and the mattress creaked.

When I was free of him, I straightened my back and my hands immediately pressed against my lower back and hips as I tried to massage the pain away. I groaned in pain and Matt offered a weak smile. His face was creased with lines of worry for his friend.

"Do you think more Hunters are going to come?" I asked.

"I sure as hell hope not. It took all I had to take care of them," Matt said. He ran his hand across his chin and his head dropped. He looked defeated and haunted, as though he had given up something of himself in that fight.

"You did well Matt. It was very impressive. If you hadn't come in-"

"I did what I had to do," he snapped in a terse voice, his head twisting around to face me. "I'm sorry, I don't mean to bite your head off. I just...I took an oath a long time ago to help people. That's why

I learned from Mom. She told me that we had to take care of people just like we take care of the world. Balance...it's all about balance...but the Hunters turn everything upside down and make us do things we thought we'd never dream of doing..."

I could sense the anguish in his voice and my heart went out to him. In a way, I thought, I was looking at him for the first time, although perhaps it was more because I had changed within myself that I was looking at things in a new way. I moved closer to him. We were both looking at Buck with worried expressions. I tugged at Matt's shirt. It was a comfort to be close to him, to know that there was someone else I could count on in all of this. I hoped that he would feel the same way about me.

"Matt I wanted to say thank you again for everything that you've done for me," I began. "Giving me the chance to speak to my parents and then saving my life and just...just being kind. I'm sorry for the way I treated you and how I betrayed your trust."

"It's okay Trish," Matt interrupted, "you've said it before. You don't need to say it again."

"No, I do," I pressed my lips together firmly and summoned a steady footing. "I didn't understand what all this meant until I spoke to my parents, and that was only possible because of you. I didn't understand my place in the world, but you did. You were honest with me and kind. You shared with me as much as you could and you tried to teach me how everything has a place in nature. You knew before I did that my place was here, and I know that too now. I'm just sorry that I had to hurt you. I don't know if I can ever repay you for what you've done for me. Without you I wouldn't be here, not in body and not in soul. You're one of the very few people who have provided me with clarity and direction in life, and you have such an impressive skill. You want to take care of people and make the world a better place. I'm sorry that I didn't appreciate that at the beginning."

I reached out and squeezed his hand. As soon as I did so his face lit up so brightly, as though I had flicked the switch to a thousand flickering lights.

"I forgive you Trish," he said, and when he looked at me I was filled with an overwhelming sense that I knew exactly what was coming next. He tilted his head to the side and leaned in. I wasn't sure. I didn't know. Part of me wanted him. I could feel myself being drawn to him, but then there was Jack and so much uncertainty. I had so many things to figure out in my own mind and heart. The easiest thing to do in that moment would have been to kiss him, but I was afraid that it would complicate my world to an even greater extent than it already was. His lips brushed mine in a light caress. Arousal and warmth spiked in my soul, but I couldn't surrender to this feeling.

Not yet.

I pulled myself away, and as I did so I immediately saw the pain flicker in his eyes, and he went rigid with tension once again. He clenched his jaw and looked away from me, focusing on Buck.

"He'll need more. I should go and prepare some for him, and more in case the others return needing treatment," he said in a numb tone. I had hurt him once before by hitting him with a thick branch, but me pulling away did more damage.

"Matt I..." I began, but what words could I have said? He shook his head and left the room. I decided I would stay there with Buck, wondering how I was getting even deeper into complication. I pulled up a chair and sat beside Buck's bed, wishing that I knew the path to keep everyone happy.

Chapter Thirteen

As I sat by Buck's bedside my mind was alive with thoughts about the battle he had fought for me. This had been the second time he had come to my rescue. The first had been with Jack and Matt in tow, but this time he had been the only thing standing in between the Hunters and me, and he'd managed to hold them off for long enough for Matt to arrive and aid him. Buck had shown so much stamina and prowess that I couldn't be mad at him, and I hoped that he would recover. Matt had left before he told me what the chances were of Buck making a recovery, but given his mood I didn't think it was a foregone conclusion. The room was small and shadows danced upon the walls. There weren't many personal touches to the room, just a single photo of a man whom I assumed to be Buck's father.

"Oh Buck, I know you can't hear me but I do hope you're going to recover. I couldn't handle it if you died because of me. This whole thing is stupid, and it's getting stupider by the second. I don't know why these Hunters want me. I'm not even that special. I know everyone thinks I am because of my father, but that's not me. I haven't done anything in my life to warrant this special treatment. I'm just a girl and I wish that everyone would stop fighting over me. All I want is a nice quiet life and for people to go around without having to be afraid that other people are going to come after them. I've already angered Matt because...oh, I don't know." I buried my head in my hands and let my hair fall about my fingers like a golden river, groaning loudly. I still hadn't figured out the specifics of my emotions and what my place in this pack was. Jack had already intimated that I needed to breed with a harem of wolves and that he couldn't keep me to himself. Did I even want that? Could I be with more than one man? Could I be with one man?

Whenever I thought of romance I always just assumed I'd meet the right person and everything would fall into place, but now that I was part of a wolf pack the previous rules went out the window. I wasn't living in a human society any longer and I couldn't hold myself to the same rules that governed them. They needed someone to breed a new generation, but part of me was still beholden to the idea of being faithful to one man. Then again...there was a deep affection in my heart for Matt as well and the way I hurt him hurt me too. It felt as though my heart was split in two already...and then there was Buck. I didn't know what my feelings for him were yet. Was it just gratitude, or was there something more? My mind was in a whirl and I felt as though I was teetering on a precipice and I had no idea where it might lead.

These anguished thoughts ran through my mind and came out in mutterings.

"Why can't there just be a simple solution to everything?" I eventually said.

"Because then it wouldn't be life," Buck replied. His voice was weak and hollow. My head snapped up and I smiled, but the smile quickly fell from my face as I saw how pale he was. I turned my head to call for Matt, but Buck placed a hand on mine and shook his head.

"I'm fine," he said, and forced a smile. He groaned and stretched out his limbs, and then groaned in pain some more. The scars and claw marks were still evident upon his flesh, joining an array of other scars that formed a pattern across his broad chest. His eyes were sunken and like two pieces of coal set in his skull.

"Buck! I'm so glad you're awake. I didn't think you'd make it. How are you feeling?"

"About as well as you can imagine, but I'll be okay. Matt came in at the nick of time."

"Yeah, he did," I smiled, although a pang of guilt erupted in my heart once again as I thought of how I had treated him and rejected the kiss he had offered with such an open heart. "Thank you Buck. Thank you for defending me. I...I don't know what would have happened had you not been here."

"They would have taken you away and prevented us from having you," Buck said. "But you're welcome. I was just doing my job."

I scowled. It had only taken moments within him regaining consciousness for me to be reminded of why he frustrated me so. My brow furrowed and I glared at him. "Oh yes, because the pack is the only thing you care about," I spat.

"Pretty much. Jack gave me orders and I followed them," he said.

I let out a dry laugh and shook my head. I couldn't believe that I had shed tears over this man, or waited by his bedside. "You really are one of a kind aren't you Buck? Isn't there anything that you care about other than the pack? Don't you ever want anything more?"

"There is nothing more," Buck replied. "And as for Matt don't worry, he'll get over it. He seems more sensitive than he actually is. As long as he gets his time among the flowers he's happy. Just be careful and make sure that what your heart wants is good for you."

"You're a philosopher now? Or just a poet," I asked, crossing my arms and sitting back, trying to put as much distance between me and him as possible. I crossed my legs as well and turned my gaze away from him. I couldn't believe that a measure of affection had actually begun to enter my heart for him, that as he was unconscious, I actually believed he was handsome. It was rare for anyone to inspire such a deep cut of emotion within me, but Buck was one of the rare ones who could do such a thing. I was also feeling vulnerable as I hadn't realized he had been listening.

"Anyway, you weren't supposed to hear that," I muttered.

Buck let out a soft laugh. "There's nobody else in the room you were talking to."

"I wasn't talking to anyone. I was just...talking. Anyway you clearly don't care about my problems so you don't need to bother yourself with thinking about them. I'm glad that you're awake. I shall take my leave of you now and go and tell Matt. Maybe he can come up with something that can put you asleep again..." I said under my breath.

"No, wait," Buck thrust out a hand and grabbed my wrist, pulling me down as I began to rise. There was an urgency to his voice that hadn't been apparent before. "I'm sorry Trish. Thank you. I'm just glad I was able to hold off the Hunters," he said in a measure of magnanimity that was sorely welcome. I tilted my head to the side and arched my eyebrows, nodding sharply in a haughty manner.

"That's all well and good, but surely you must know that you can't go through life this way. If you really believe that nothing matters but the pack, what if the pack gets destroyed?"

"As long as one of us survives, so does the pack," Buck said through gritted teeth. "It's not something an outsider would understand." He leaned his head back on the pillow and closed his eyes. The way he addressed me as an outsider so casually stung me more than I thought it would.

"Have you forgotten? I'm not an outsider," I said.

"You may have the blood of the wolf, but that doesn't make you one. Jack has deluded himself because he sees what he wants to see when he looks at you, and he's never going to get over the hero worship of Jake. Matt is too soft to doubt anything. But you and I both know that you're not your father. You said it yourself. You don't know why people keep treating you like you're special. Maybe the cold hard truth is that you're not."

I hadn't been prepared to hear the doubts in my mind vocalized so forcefully and so bluntly. My mouth hung open, agape, not quite sure what to say to that. Buck had a way of getting under my skin that was unrivalled by anyone aside from perhaps my Mom, and he certainly didn't have her privilege in getting away with it.

"I don't know why you think you have the freedom to talk to me like this, but you don't. You might not agree with me being here, but the fact is I am here, and I'm going to be here for a while longer so you'll have to get used to it. What happened to you Buck? What made you like this? For someone who values the pack over everything else you're very quick to push people away, or is it that you don't care about the pack at all; you only care about yourself."

I could bite back as hard as he could. He snarled and his upper lip curled. I have no doubt that if he had been stronger he would have risen from the bed and paced angrily around the room, perhaps even smashing his fist into the door. As it was he stayed rooted to the bed, his body betraying him for a rare moment in his life.

"You have no idea what you're talking about," he said, and turned his head away from me.

"Oh no? Then maybe that man does?" I pointed to the picture on the wall. Even though Buck didn't turn to face me I knew he knew what I was pointing to. His face remained impassive and he breathed in slowly, trying to keep himself calm, but my blood was raging. I was tired of how he could get to me so easily and how he always seemed to say the wrong thing. "You can try and tell me otherwise Buck, but clearly you're just a selfish person who only cares about his own self-preservation. I thought for a moment I had seen something different inside you, but now I see that was just a lie. Maybe you don't know what it means to be a part of a pack at all."

That certainly got to the heart of the matter. He twisted his entire body around and seemed to internalize the pain he must have been in as he didn't cry out or even flinch, and I knew he must have been in a lot of pain as he moved far more quickly than he should have. His dark, bloodshot eyes stared at me with the pain of an anguished soul and a dark cloud swirled around his mind. When he spoke he hissed at me. There was no slanting smile to be seen. No cocky smirk. All the natural ease with which he conducted himself was absent and he was just a man in emotional turmoil.

"I am nothing like that man. The pack is the only thing that matters to me. It's the only thing that has ever mattered to me. Don't you dare insult me by speaking about matters that you don't understand."

The vehemence of his reaction was more than I expected and it actually made a sliver of fear creep through my body. I flinched and realized that I had pushed him too far without properly understanding why. After what happened with Matt it seemed as though I was on a run of insulting the wolves closest to me, and I wondered how long it would be before I did the same to Jack, although in that case the opposite had taken effect as I didn't appreciate the way he had left me without saying anything. We needed to have words when he got back; that was playing on my mind too and everything else came out in this wave of awkward emotion.

But it wasn't fair. As much as Buck was irascible and drove me crazy he had still put his life on the line for me and what I said about him being selfish was blatantly untrue. He had proven that to me twice and I wanted to take back my words.

"I didn't mean it Buck. I know that's not true, but I don't know why you're so defensive towards me. Tell me what made you react like that," I said.

Buck remained silent for a few moments and I wondered if he was going to speak to me again at all. The tension in the room was terse and I wasn't sure how much more of it I could take, but I wanted to persevere. Despite everything that seemed to go against it, a connection had formed between us. As much as he drove me crazy I couldn't help but think of the way he fought for me, the way he had bled for me, and the way he had almost died for me. That meant something deep and profound, and I wasn't about to let it go easily.

Thankfully, neither was he, it seemed.

*

"You're not the only one who had some issues with their father," he said. "That man raised me, but I never paid attention to any lesson he tried to teach me."

"Why not? What happened?"

"He tried to teach me all the wrong lessons. I know you probably had some idea of what my life was like from the very first moment we met, but I can guarantee you it's wrong. I was like any other kid, growing up with a mom and a dad in a nice house in the suburbs. Mom was sweet and the house was always filled with the smell of something baking or cooking. Dad worked a nine to five job, always had time for me, always helped me with my homework and spent time with me over the weekend. We went to ball games, we watched movies together, it was basically a patchwork of every idyllic childhood that has ever existed."

"Then what was so wrong with it?"

"It was all a lie," Buck said bitterly. There was a haunted look to his eyes as his gaze drifted past me to the photo on the wall, and then he continued his story. "For a time I thought that nothing was different about me. I was a little bigger than the other boys, stronger and faster, but mom and dad just said that was because I ate my vegetables and didn't stuff myself with candy. But I knew that something inside me was different, I just didn't know what it was yet. As I grew up I became more confused. I seemed angry all the time and I could sense things that others couldn't. The world seemed brighter to me, and when I tried explaining it to my friends they told me that I was making things up. And when it came to playing at school I was too good. Everything was too easy for me because of my natural advantages. I dominated everything, so much so that it was unfair to the other kids, so none of them wanted to play with me. I was an outcast and I didn't understand why nobody else could see the world the same way that I knew it.

And then I became a teenager. I started getting angrier. My temper was out of control. I got into fights at school and, of course, I never lost them, but it felt like everything was falling apart around me. I was the only thing that had changed, so I knew that somehow it had to be my fault, but I didn't understand what I could do to stop it. I was only doing what came naturally to me, and yet somehow that was wrong."

He paused for a moment. Knowing what I knew of Buck I doubted if he told these things to many people, and I remained quiet for fear that if I spoke I would interrupt him and never get the opportunity again, as though a rare bird had landed in front of me and I dared not move in case it grew frightened and flew away. I let Buck continue with his story. But I got a sense of his pain and I identified with the loneliness he must have felt. My heart began to warm to him as he opened up to me.

"One day Dad called me into the basement. He was rifling through a box and pulled out that old photo. He seemed different than usual and I thought I was in trouble. I guess I was, but not in the way that I thought." Buck licked his dry lips. Matt had left some water in here so I lifted some to Buck's lips and carefully tilted the glass up so as not to spill it all down his chin. Buck swallowed and then continued talking.

"He started telling me that he'd had another life before I came into the world, and that he'd tried to keep it separate from my life as much as possible, but there was no way to do so any longer. He told me all about the kind of magic in the world and how we had been blessed by Mother Moon, and that I was a werewolf, just like him. I didn't believe it at first. I thought he was having me on and I was ready to leave him there, when he shifted in front of me. I couldn't believe it, but as soon as I saw it, I knew it made sense and I was hungry for the knowledge. I asked him everything and we stayed up all night. It was the first time in a long time that Dad and I had shared something like that, and it really reminded me of what my childhood was like, but at the same time I started to resent him because he had kept this a secret from me and I didn't understand why.

He told me that it was getting to the point when I would start shifting and that, especially in the turbulent teenage years, it was going to be difficult to control my instincts, but that as I grew up and matured it would get easier, and eventually I would be able to blend into society like he did and have a normal life. But I was already thinking to myself, why would I want a normal life when I could be a wolf? I asked him if there were more of us out there and a strange look came over him. I could tell that he didn't really want to talk about it, but I was so insistent that he didn't really have a choice. Once he'd opened the can of worms there was no way he could stop them from spilling out. He told me all about the motorcycle club and the pack, and how he had once belonged. I'll always remember the way he spoke about it, with such a wistful tone in his voice. Anyway, I asked him what happened to them. I figured something must have happened otherwise we'd still be there. Dad went quiet. He told me about the Hunters, and that he didn't think it was safe anymore. He told me that when he found out Mom was pregnant with me he made plans to leave and I just...I couldn't understand it. If the pack was in danger then surely his place was with them, to protect them? But no, Dad thought of himself and his family first. He put my safety over that of the pack and he left them weaker. He gave up the nobility of being a wolf for a safe life in a safe city where the only thing he had to worry about was his son learning his secret.

And as soon as I found out what he'd done I hated him. I couldn't believe that he would betray his own people like that. In the same breath as he told me that the pack was the most important thing to a wolf, he also told me that he had left them when they needed help the most. He tried to make me feel better by saying that mom and I were his new pack, but I knew it was just something he told himself to make himself feel better. I thought of all the people that I couldn't help because I hadn't known they existed, and I thought about everything that had been denied to me. I burned with anger when I realized what he'd done, how he'd betrayed my nobility as a wolf, even before I had been born. I had to get away, I had to get back to my roots and reclaim my heritage. I had to make up for what Dad had done, so I did some more digging and found out about this place. When I got here, I found out that Dad wasn't the only one who had left. The wolves had let fear ruin them and had fled to pastures new, but I wasn't about to let the same thing happen. I joined them, leaving my old life behind. The life that Dad had tried to forge for me, had tried to present to me as a gift. But I didn't want it. It was cursed. As soon as I came here I swore that I would do anything I could to serve this pack, to serve Jack. And I keep that picture there to remind me that I'll never turn into someone like him. I'll never turn my back on the pack," his words were harsh and heavy with emotion.

When he finally finished talking, Buck took a deep breath that made his chest rise high, and for a moment I thought he had exhausted himself completely. His story struck a chord with me as I had obviously had a fractured relationship with my own mother, and I could well imagine the betrayal he must have felt when he realized that his father had been lying to him for his entire life. But one thing struck me as incredibly sad.

"And you've never been back to see him since?"

"Never," Buck said, without a hint of regret in his voice. I looked at the man with a new sense of pity. He was clearly in pain and not just from the attack. The pain ran deep, through his skin and bones, right down into his soul. His had been a lifetime of trying to correct a mistake, a mistake that wasn't his.

"Buck," I said gently, not wanting to irritate him further. "I know it's difficult, but we can't define ourselves by our parents. I spent a lot of my life living in my mom's shadow and I ended up turning away from what she wanted me to be because she tried so hard to make that into my destiny. You can't spend your life trying to fix your father's mistake. It's not your job. And I know that it's not easy to face a parent when you find out they're not perfect, but he's still your father and it's important to remember that while he's a wolf, he's still only human. I've had problems with both of my parents and I wish that I had been able to speak to them more while they had been alive. I never got a chance to meet my Dad and in her later years my relationship with Mom had been so difficult that we never spoke as a mother and daughter should. I know the pack is important, but family is important too and there should always be a chance for people to make it right. Maybe in time you could see your father again. Sometimes it's hard to understand why people do things but we have to look at things from other people's perspective to try and understand them. That's what I did with you wolves. If I hadn't I'd never have been able to forgive you for taking me away from my life."

"I have seen it from his perspective," Buck said, tearing his gaze away from the photo. "And I hate it, because it makes me feel like a coward."

"He's still your father, and one day you're going to want to talk to him, but you're not going to be able to. Even though I knew that Mom was dying of cancer I never got a chance to tell her all the things I wanted to tell her. There's always something more to say. Maybe if he sees what you've done with your life he might change the way he lives and be better for it."

"Maybe," he growled. I figured it was a sign of progress at least and rather than being turned away by his rough manner and his curt tone, my heart opened up to him. I wanted to help him. This was a man who had been betrayed by his family, who had discovered that his father didn't abide by the values that he had taught to Buck, and now the pack was all that Buck had. He claimed to not care about anything else, but I knew that wasn't true. He just didn't let himself care. I had a sense of what the underlying issue was because I had been through the same thing, although I didn't voice it at the time because he wasn't ready to hear it and he'd only have denied it anyway. Perhaps in time I would share it with him, when we had a deeper connection. But the issue was that he was afraid of turning into his father, afraid that if he had a family he might leave the pack he claimed to love so much. He came here to fix his father's mistake, but he was paralyzed by the fear of repeating that mistake. I was exactly the same; always so afraid that I would end up like my mother and expect my children to follow a path that had been denied to me.

I pressed a hand to his arm and squeezed it gently, deciding that now was the best time to leave.

"Thank you again Buck," I said, and leaned forward to offer him an affectionate kiss. The gesture took him by surprise and he mumbled something in reply, before he turned away from me and continued to rest. I took a last look at him before I left the room, confused by the swirl of emotions that ran through my mind.

Chapter Fourteen

I left Buck and despite being in there for a little while, Jack and the other wolves had not yet returned. Although it was awkward I knew I had to find Matt and talk to him, not just about Buck, but about what had happened between us. I walked back into the bar and found him cleaning up. He had taken the dead wolves away and was in the process of sweeping up glass and righting the tables and chairs. I walked up and helped him. When he saw me he stiffened and averted his gaze. He didn't make any attempt to speak to me.

"Buck's awake," I said.

"That's good," he replied. I bent down to pick up a chair and watched Matt. I wasn't entirely sure how to broach the subject with him. I wanted to try and reassure him, but there was so much uncertainty in my mind I had no idea where to really begin. When I thought of the three men, I had so much affection for all three of them, and in such different ways as well. My feelings towards them were all different, but had the same intensity.

"Shouldn't the others have been back by now?" I asked.

"I suppose so, but you never know with the Hunters. I just hope they all end up coming back. If they don't then this is all over." His words dripped with despair and his eyes were haunted. Matt was the one that had seemed to be upbeat and chipper, but his mood had darkened. I wasn't sure how much my rejection had played a part in that. Perhaps it was being egotistical of me to even imagine that I was important enough to have played a part, but I couldn't help it.

"Don't speak like that Matt. We can't think like that. It'll be okay. Jack will bring them back."

Matt winced as I mentioned Jack's name, although he didn't respond.

"Matt, about earlier," I continued, "I'm sorry-"

"It's okay. You don't have to be sorry. This is just the way it goes. Jack is the leader after all. It makes sense."

"No I-"

"Honestly Trish it's okay," he had a mean look on his face as he shrugged his shoulders and shook his head, pretending that he didn't care. "This is just the way it goes. I should have expected it really. When Jack said he wanted to make the pack strong I figured that what he really meant was that he wanted a mate. I tried not to fall for you at the start, but I couldn't help myself. I could tell you were different and that day when we went walking in the meadow...I feel pathetic for saying it, but it might well have been the happiest day of my life. All I want is to protect people and keep them safe. I'm just a healer and I suppose I'll have to find my happiness elsewhere. I'll be able to stop caring about you like this in a while. I just need to let the pain subside first. I'll need some space, but I'll be okay. You don't have to feel guilty about being with Jack or being the mother this pack needs."

The way he said those last few words struck a chord with me. Being the mother to the pack was a role of which I had not fully grasped the magnitude. I wasn't just here for breeding, I was here to take care of them, to love them and help guide them to a new beginning, a new future. And I knew in that moment that I couldn't limit my heart to Jack. As much as I felt a deep attraction and connection to him it was a crime against my own soul to ignore my desires. Jack had brought me here to save the pack and take care of the pack. I couldn't stand by while Matt felt this way and not share some of my feelings with him.

I moved closer and tugged at his shirt to get him to turn around. When he did, I saw the redness of his eyes. His voice had been raw with emotion when he had spoken. I made sure my voice was gentle and caring.

"Matt, I care about you deeply and you have meant so much to me. You're the one who first showed me kindness, who trusted me even though it went against your better judgment. This place, this pack...it has become obsessed with the past and it is a place of fear and darkness. They need you perhaps more than anyone to show them that there is a better way. We can both heal them, together. What's more is that you allowed me to speak with my parents. You helped me break the laws of the world. You helped me do the impossible and I couldn't ever deny that this means so much to me."

I lifted my hand and placed it against his cheek. He leaned into me instinctively and I was overwhelmed with a warm feeling that swelled in the pit of my stomach and ran through every part of my body. I felt a pull towards him, the same kind of pull that I felt to Jack, although it was slightly different too. The nuances were difficult to explain and in the moment I wasn't thinking anything about that, I just knew that I wanted to make Matt happy and for him to feel like he could trust me again, especially to trust me with his heart. I moved my hand to where it rested against the back of his head and pulled him down towards me. His thick hair was soft against my fingers and his hands came around my waist, lifting me onto my tiptoes. When our lips met, the kiss was tender and deep, and I could feel the longing that had been within him from the first moment we met. My eyes closed and I drowned in his embrace, wrapping my arms around his neck, feeling the tingling sensations rushing through my body.

I knew it was the right decision from the moment our lips met because I wasn't filled with a sense of guilt or that this was wrong. It felt natural to kiss Matt, just as it had felt natural to be with Jack and I was intrigued by the possibilities. I thought it was no wonder that I had never been able to fit into the normal world if deep down I had always wanted a life like this. It was clear to me now that I had just been treading water until my real life had begun.

The kiss grew deeper and his hold on me became tighter. It may well have led to more had that not been the moment when the other wolves returned.

Chapter Fifteen

The roar of motorcycles came thundering down the road. We had been so lost in our kiss that neither Matt nor I broke away until we saw them pulling up outside the bar, the smoke rising from the engines in a thick cloud, momentarily covering the landscape. The doors burst open and Jack walked in, his face like thunder. As soon as he saw Matt and I standing so close together with our arms around each other he stormed into the middle of the room, fists clenched by his sides. My hands fell away from Matt, and he stepped back slowly. The warmth of his touch slipped away from my waist and I was cold again.

Although I didn't feel any guilt there was a part of me that was shocked by the sense of being caught and panic flared inside me, not because I thought I was doing anything wrong, but because I wasn't sure how Jack would react.

"What's going on here?" he asked, his voice terse, his body tense. The other members of the pack started filtering in through the door and their voices hushed as they realized that something was afoot.

"There was an attack," Matt said in a wavering voice. "The Hunters came while you were gone. Buck and I managed to fight them off, but Buck's in a pretty bad way. He's recovering now." We both knew that wasn't what Jack had meant. His eye twitched and he glanced back at the rest of the pack. I got the feeling that he wanted to confront us about what had been going on, but he couldn't risk being so petty in front of the pack, not when the clubhouse had been attacked. Jack shifted his glance between Matt and me, and then barked an order for the others to help clean up before he marched out of the room. I glanced at Matt, who offered me a shrug, and suddenly the future was clouded again. The thought of loving three men came easily to me, but juggling the emotions of all of them was going to be difficult.

"I'll talk to him," I whispered, and followed Jack's path to his room.

*

"I'm not sure you should be here right now. I might say something I will regret," he said as soon as I entered, even though he had his back to the door. Sometimes their enhanced senses really annoyed me.

"I think we need to talk."

"Do you? About what?"

"Well, first about why you left me this morning without saying anything. I woke up and you were gone, only to find out that you had gone to speak with the Hunters. You might have died Jack. What if you had left without saying goodbye?"

"I thought you'd understand. I didn't want to worry you unduly," Jack said.

"It doesn't work like that. You have to be open and honest with me. You can't spend the night with someone and then just leave without saying anything."

"Is that why you feel justified in kissing Matt? I can still smell him on you, you know."

Those damned wolf senses. I clenched my jaw and tried to quell the anger that was rising within me as I didn't want it to overwhelm me. I didn't want to lose control. I was confused and tired, and all I wanted was to know where I stood.

"What do you want from me Jack? What did you expect to happen? You said you wanted me to help bring the pack back to greatness, to use my lineage to make the pack strong again. If that's the case then I'm going to need to be with more than you. That's just the nature of the bargain."

"But it doesn't mean you have to love all of them," Jack hissed. I was stunned for a moment by the intensity imbued in his voice, but I was also shaken by his vulnerability. For a man who was so strong and so authoritative, so confident and commanding, his emotional state was shaky and he felt things deeply. The anger evaporated as I saw him in a new light, and love flowed through me instead, making my voice gentle. The atmosphere in the room shifted and the tension began to dissipate, but it was clear that we had some talking to do. We had rushed into sleeping together, into surrendering to our desires and passion, without thinking about the ramifications. I wondered if the same thing had happened with my parents, if my father had ever thought twice about falling in love with Mom because of what he was and because of what loving him meant for her. Some things were just inexorable though.

"Jack...you can't expect me not to love them. I'm not going to be able to give my heart to you and my body to everyone else, that's not how I work. I need to be free to love who I want, and if I am going to bear children then I want to be able to choose the fathers myself. I know now that my place is here. I have accepted that fully and I will not fight it, but there are certain conditions. I have deep feelings for you Jack and I cannot fight the attraction, but I know I am meant for more than simply being the mate of the alpha. This pack...it is hurting. The wolves in it are hurting and I have come to try and soothe them. I'm sure with your senses you can see the pain that surrounds each of you. I want to help, but if we are to breed a new generation of wolves then they are going to need different qualities. This pack needs your leadership skills, but it also needs Buck's strength, and Matt's compassion. Don't you see that you are all the sum parts that make a great whole, and with me in the middle of it we can breed strong wolves, but it needs everyone to be happy with the way things work out. There can be no room for jealousy or envy, or for feelings of possession."

As I said this Jack's head twisted around and he glared at me. I knew I had struck a nerve but now was not the time to be coy with my words. My place in this world was becoming clearer to me with every passing moment and the clarity was welcomed within my soul. I braced myself for a barrage of emotional words, a torrent of jealousy that he needed to get out of his system but, thankfully, he calmed himself before he spoke.

"Such a thing has been known to happen in the past," he said. "The wolves lost their way as the world moved on. We fooled ourselves into thinking we were like the other humans and suffered from the same trappings. We lived like them, one mate, one family, but we have always been a pack. You are right. I...I apologize for my outburst. I suppose there are lingering feelings of resentment because of what happened before. I already had one woman I loved taken from me and when I saw you and Matt I had the distinct feeling it was happening again."

I smiled at him. "I wasn't being taken from you Jack. Just because I have feelings for Matt does not change my feelings for you. It is like children or parents, we can love more than one of them. Romantic love should be no different, it is no different, at least not for me. I understand that now and I understand my role in the pack. But it is not only me you should apologize to. Matt did not deserve your ire."

Jack glowered as I said this, but he nodded in numb acceptance. "I will make it right with him. This is the best way to make the pack stronger," he said, as though he was talking himself into accepting the way I wanted things to be. Relief washed over me as I felt the pieces falling into place and I couldn't stop my mouth from curling into a smile.

"So are Matt and Buck the others you have chosen?" he asked. Hearing the question put like that was striking and I almost deferred my answer, but I realized I needed no more time to decide. My feelings for Jack and Matt were deep, and Buck...well, there was something about him that made my heart cry out in pity and I wanted to show him that it was possible to love something other than the pack. I dipped my head as I nodded and replied in the affirmative, sealing my fate, promising myself to these three men, these wolves. Excitement and anticipation flickered within like a burning flame. I didn't know where this decision was going to take me, but I was certain it was the correct one. The wolves held a special place in my heart and I knew I belonged here. Like my father before me I would lead these wolves into a new era, I would protect them as best I could and I would fill their lives with love.

I had never made a positive decision like this before, not one that would define the course of my life. The only other major decision I had made was a negative one, to not go into the same career as my mother wanted. A flood of pure joy filled me as I welcomed this sensation of love into my heart, as I welcomed these three men into my soul. I knew I would never be in command of them and I would never ever direct the journey of the pack, but to have them be a part of me and to play a part in their lives, to offer them love and strong children filled me with a sense of purpose and I knew that I was at home.

"We should all talk about this," Jack said, "but first there is something that must be taken care of."

My heart sank instantly as it felt as though he had ripped away my idea of paradise. But a chill crept down my spine at the tone of his voice. His body took on a defensive posture and I realized that with all this talk of emotion there was still one thing that I hadn't asked him, and that was how his meeting with the Hunters went. With them still lurking I knew there wasn't any way for us to be happy because they would always be there, trying to tear us down and ruin our happiness, to try and stop us from living our best lives. I had seen how determined they were to get to me and to stop us from being strong, and pure, unadulterated hatred ran through my mind.

"We need to stop them," I said.

"That's what I'm planning to do," Jack said.

*

Jack and I emerged from his room and returned to the bar, where everyone apart from Buck was tidying up the mess that the Hunters had made. The men were in good spirits as Matt had evidently shared with them the story of what had happened in their absence and they reveled in the glory of battle. I could see that they had drinks in their hands and were toasting the resolve of Buck and Matt. When we entered there was a great cheer that erupted, one I assumed was for Jack, but actually it was for me.

"I told them about the way you fended off the wolf," Matt said.

I blushed and nodded. Frankly I didn't think I had done anything heroic since I had just cowered behind the bar and surviving had been a matter of fortune more than anything else, but I took their congratulations in my stride and was glad that they didn't just see me as a weak female. Matt glanced with tension at Jack, and Jack betrayed no emotion. I offered Matt a warm smile to say that everything was going to be okay, although I didn't know if he believed me at that moment. Jack strode into the middle of the room and was handed a glass of whiskey, which he took and slugged back, before slamming the glass down on a table. The bubble of chatter died down as all attention was focused on him. I shifted beside Matt, who looked uncomfortable, no doubt worried that Jack would look at him in enmity again.

"It's okay," I whispered to Matt, "I need to talk with you after all this. I know why I'm here. I know what I want to do with this pack," I said. I wished that I could have been more specific or at least hinted to more of an idea of what would happen in the future. I still had to see if Matt and Buck would even be happy sharing my affection and had to tell myself that the future had not been written yet, even if it made so much sense in my mind. There had been so much talk of destiny and I was not yet ready to accept that everything was laid out in a set sequence. Just because I wanted something badly, because I could foresee something working in my mind, didn't mean that it was going to happen without any difficulty. There was a chance that neither Matt nor Buck would be interested in the kind of arrangement that I wanted. If that was the case then I would have to adjust my plans fully. It might be the case that I ended up with Jack and only Jack, and although I loved the man, that prospect did not seem as wonderful as the alternative.

But, as it was, I had to leave Matt in mystery for a little while longer as Jack commanded the attention of the entire pack and began to speak.

"Today was a dark day, as the Hunters dared to attack our clubhouse. They're getting more aggressive and more confident. So far we've managed to fight them off, but if they keep attacking we're only going to be able to hold out for a certain amount of time. Buck almost died today, and I know that if we keep doing what we're doing it's only a matter of time before they storm us with everything they have, and there will be a slaughter. We went there today with two things in mind. I wanted to hear what their offer of peace was, if indeed it was genuine. I knew in my heart that it wouldn't be, so I wasn't surprised to find they were stalling while their hunting party came here to try and take Trish from us. But we did learn a lot. They're not as powerful as they seem, and they haven't made good use of the community. They live in squalor. Instead of building something worthwhile, something they can be proud of, they've been scavenging off the land and they're getting desperate. They are an example of what happens when wolves lose their way. They're barely better than wild wolves, untamed, living on instinct, and that is why we are going to win. We're smarter than them, and we know what it is to live in a community. We have enjoyed the best of both worlds, human and wolf, and that is what is going to give us the advantage.

We're going to go back there and reclaim our home. We're going to show the Hunters that their way is not best, and we're going to restore pride to our pack. We're going to make it so that everyone who left out of fear will return, and our pack will grow strong again. For too long we have been living in the darkness, shackled to the despair that came before us. Tragedy has struck so many times and it is only natural that we should be afraid of those that wish to destroy us, but that time is over. Today is the first day of the rest of our lives and I say that we are going to have long lives. We are going to take back what was once ours, and we're going to prove once and for all that the Howlers are the best damned pack of wolves that there has ever been!"

His voice rose into a crescendo and it crashed throughout the entire clubhouse. The other wolves raised their drinks and cheered and hollered, spellbound by Jack's words and I was once again reminded of when he mentioned that there was magic in the world. I saw it before me in the way he commanded and inspired the pack. I felt it myself too, my skin tingled and prickles rose in small bubbles over my arms. Breath caught in my throat and my skin became flushed as arousal drew me towards him. If there had been nobody else there I would have torn off his clothes and flung myself at him, but I managed to control myself in the midst of the other wolves.

When the cacophony of the war cry subsided, Jack addressed them again, this time in a low and deliberate voice, and that displayed his keen mind and showed why he was the leader of the pack.

"Tonight, in the darkness, we're going to run as wolves through the night as a pack, and then we're going to set up traps all around their camp to help give us an advantage. We're going to have to be quiet and we're going to have to work quickly so as not to be discovered. In the morning we'll attack before they even expect it. They won't think that we would dare to be so brazen and they'll be arrogant. The traps will take out a great number of them, and we'll take care of the rest. By the time we're finished with them the Hunters will be no more and they'll flee into the wilderness, their tails between their legs."

Someone asked how they were going to get to the small town without being detected, as the Hunters would surely have been able to smell them. I was glad that someone asked the question as I was wondering the same thing myself. Jack smirked and I knew that he had a plan. He cocked an eyebrow and looked to Matt.

"Our resident healer has been working on something," he said, and gestured to Matt. Matt stepped forward and cleared his throat, before pulling a small vial out of his pocket.

"I call this Whisper," he said, and explained that once drunk it would mask their scent for some time.

Jack smiled with pride. "This is going to allow us to creep up close to them and set our traps. They'll never see us coming. They might have the numerical advantage over us, but they don't have the ingenuity. Matt's been working on a few other potions as well to increase our strength and endurance. They'll only last a short time though, so we must make sure that we make the time count!"

I looked at Matt, a little surprised that he hadn't shared any of this with me, but he merely shrugged. I was glad to see that the other wolves congratulated him and thanked him and valued him. It would have been easy for them all to look down upon him because he was just a healer, but even though he was not the strongest wolf he could still offer them a lot in combat and they depended on him. Jack explained the plan in more detail and I listened intently as he talked about setting various traps around the perimeter of the small town, and then they would draw the Hunters out in an initial flurry to take out as many of them as they could, before engaging them in battle.

It was natural for the wolves to get excited about the thought of testing their mettle in battle, so the mood in the bar was one of excitement and anticipation, but as Jack described the plan and spoke about the number of the Hunters it became clear that this was not going to have a happy ending for everyone. It was a deadly battle and people were going to die; people that could include the ones I loved. My heart sank as I thought about a future without them and tears welled in my eyes as a deep sadness clutched my heart. They had to come back, they just had to. I knew that the Hunters could not be reasoned with, could not be bargained with. They were vile wolves who had killed my father and many other wolves all for the sake of proving themselves more powerful, and it was time that they were taught a lesson.

I looked at Jack with pride as he explained the plan, but I was also filled with worry at what the future might hold. As much as I knew we were on the right side of justice that didn't always mean victory was assured and the night would be filled with anxiety and worry on my part. I had to talk to them before they left. I wanted to tell them what I wanted from the future, in the hope that it would inspire them to fight even harder, and I didn't want any of them to die before they knew how I felt.

Chapter Sixteen

Once Jack had finished speaking there was a convivial mood as the pack looked forward to battle. There were only a few hours until nightfall, so the wolves went about their business and rested before they were due to leave. As soon as Jack and Matt were both free, for they were inundated with attention after Jack declared his plan, I got them to come with me to Buck's room. Buck was looking a little more alert, although he was still in pain. He propped himself up into a sitting position and was eager to learn about what had happened with the Hunters. I waited patiently while Jack and Matt quickly explained to him what was happening. Color had returned to his face and he was looking much more alive than he had been before. I was amazed by the rate at which he healed. There was no end to the wonder that came with the supernatural abilities of the wolves, although I had to put my awe aside so that I could talk with them.

"I have spoken with Jack about this, but I wanted to gather you all here before you go and fight the Hunters just so that we know what can happen when you return. My father was important to this pack and the tragedy of his death has rippled through the years. Only now I feel the pack is beginning to recover. You took me away from my life because you thought that I could be the mother to a new generation of wolves, one that will be strong and compassionate," I looked at each of the men in turn as I said this. "At first I didn't understand what I could even offer all of you, but the more time I've spent with you the more I've realized that this is the place where I belong. I want to be the mother to a new generation, but I'm not going to be the property of one man and I'm not going to be beholden to the entire pack either. I've made a connection with each of you and I cannot ignore the feelings in my heart. In some cases I know, and in some cases I hope, that you feel the same way I do. I want us all to be a little pack of our own. I want to have your children and to raise them into being strong wolves. I know it's not conventional, but I cannot deny my feelings for you and I do not want to deny them. Go and win this fight against the Hunters and when you return we shall celebrate properly," there was a gleaming promise in my eyes as I looked at each of them in turn.

Jack turned to Matt and apologized for the way he had reacted earlier. Matt accepted it without any hesitation.

"I think I could get used to this," Buck said with a hungry look in his eyes, a look that seemed to strip away all my clothes and left me exposed and vulnerable, "but you're asking a lot for us all to come back without being harmed."

"It's not asking too much in your case, is it? Surely you won't be fighting?" I asked in reply. Buck frowned and pushed himself up even more, looking towards Jack.

"You're going to need your best fighter. You can't seriously be thinking about keeping me back here?"

"You've had a heavy day..." Jack said, "maybe it is for the best that you rest."

Buck scoffed. "I've never missed a fight and I'm not planning to miss the most important one this pack has ever fought. You're going to plant the traps tonight and then fight in the morning, right? Well, Matt can just come up with some concoction that'll help me heal through the night and I'll come in like a wrecking ball in the morning. I have to repay them for what they did to me today," he growled. The sheer determination in his voice wasn't something any of us wanted to argue with and although I worried about him going into battle in his condition I knew that it was a part of his nature to fight. I could no more ask him to stay behind than I could ask myself not to breathe.

"What about me?" I asked in a small voice. The men glanced at each other.

"You should stay here," Jack said.

"I'm afraid I don't have anything that can make you more resilient. The potions I have will only work on wolves," Matt added.

"We won't be long. We'll come back and then we can sort all of this out," Jack said, trying to be reassuring but I think he could see that the idea of staying here while they all went out to fight was troubling. "You won't be in danger here. They won't know we're coming. The only traps that are being set this time are the ones we're setting. All you'll have to do is wait."

"You make it sound so easy," I said wryly, when in fact it was probably one of the most difficult things he could have asked me to do. How could I sit there and wait while the wolves risked their lives, not knowing which one of them survived and which were in danger of dying? I could drive myself crazy with fear, and yet at the same time I knew there was nothing else I could do. I wasn't strong enough to fight alongside them and I'd only be a hindrance. Sacrifices were needed, and in this case I had to sacrifice my own sanity. I took a deep breath and ran my hand through my hair, pushing my hair back, revealing my face. "I'll be waiting when you return," I said.

*

At least I had been able to speak with them. I felt relieved because of this and I was looking forward to the future when we could all be together properly. I had to believe that we would all be together. I couldn't cope with the idea that any of them would die before I got a chance to explore my feelings for them properly.

Although the mood around the clubhouse was one of anticipation, it was laced with tension as well. People knew that if anything went wrong the likelihood was that it was going to cost them their lives, but if this was going to be their last night on earth they were going to make sure it was a damned good one. As twilight began to set in and the day turned to dusk there was a great feast laid out, laden with meat that would give them the strength to last the night and fight through the morning. They sang songs and shared tales regarding battles of old to give them inspiration. They talked about other wolves that had died in heroic circumstances and each of them was ready to etch their name in history. There was a great cheer when Buck staggered out of his room to make an appearance at the feast and they all congratulated him for his efforts in fending off the vicious Hunters. I looked at my wolves with great affection and although I was not in communion with him, I prayed to my father to watch over them and guide them however he could.

Eventually it came time for the wolves to leave. The moon was high in the sky, the stars twinkled brightly, and the night was cool and clear. One by one they drank the potion that would mask their scent, and then they moved outside, all except for Buck, who drank a different potion and returned to his room to rest, after wishing them good luck. I walked to the door as the pack mustered outside by their motorcycles. Jack came to me and promised me that he would return. Matt offered me a warm smile, promising the same thing, and I made sure to look at them closely in case this was the last time I would ever see them. I etched their faces into my memory and suppressed the sorrow that threatened to rise within me. I could not stop the tide of fear flowing through my mind. The pack turned and faced the open road. One by one they shifted into wolves and it was one of the most beautiful sights I had ever seen. There were a dozen or so of them. They lifted their heads and howled, and my heart was moved by this primal sound. They moved as one as they streaked away into the night, disappearing into the darkness. There was nothing for me to do but wait and wonder how many of them would return.

Chapter Seventeen

I returned inside to the empty clubhouse. Buck had returned to bed. I tried to keep myself busy by cleaning up the bar, but it didn't do much to take my mind off of things. I shot a few balls around the pool table and tried watching some TV, but all I could think about were the wolves putting their lives in danger against the Hunters, and I couldn't help but feel that they were doing so for me. The Hunters had made it their mission to prevent me from helping breed a new generation of Howlers. If I hadn't been here perhaps their attacks wouldn't have been so fierce. I suppose there was no point in blaming myself when attacks would have come anyway, but I knew that I was a part of the tapestry and I was more annoyed at not being able to help than anything else. It was so frustrating to be the daughter of the wolf and not have any of the other qualities that made them so special.

Since I couldn't concentrate, I returned to my room and tried to sleep, but my mind was alive with worry and I couldn't relax. Whenever I closed my eyes I was taken back to that earlier moment when the wolf had leapt towards me and snarled at me. I was paralyzed by the look of threat in his eyes and they seemed to stare at me beyond the veil of the physical world. Even though the wolf was dead, its form still haunted me, and I knew that if Jack and Matt failed the rest would come for me eventually, although by that point I would have nothing left to live for.

I tried to surrender to sleep but the walls felt cavernous and the moon outside was so far away. I felt alone, and my inner anguish echoed in the stillness of the night. I couldn't bear being alone, so I dragged myself to Buck's room and opened the door carefully. Silver light slanted in through a window and illuminated his body. The blanket was draped over his middle, revealing his scarred body. He stirred and murmured something as I moved to the bed and peeled the blanket away, slipping in beside him.

"I don't want to be alone Buck. Not tonight," I said in a fragile whisper, "please just let me stay here," I asked.

He shifted over to make room and wrapped his arms around me. I sobbed a little as I embraced him, but quickly felt better as his strength soothed me. My hair fell against his shoulder and I reached over his body to hold him. The powerful thrum of his heartbeat lulled me to sleep. As my hand slid over his body my fingers felt the crisscrossing pattern of scars and I thought to myself that if he had survived so much already then he could survive this as well, just as much as the others could. I managed to sleep as I held him tightly, managed to push aside the terrors of my mind because I wasn't alone. I was with him.

*

Morning rose and I awoke with Buck. The sunlight poured into the room and I rubbed my eyes, immediately wondering about the others.

"I wonder how they're getting on," I said.

"I don't know, but I'm going to find out," Buck pulled himself out of bed and pulled on a shirt. He was still moving a little more stiffly than usual.

"Are you sure you're going to be okay for this?" I asked.

"I'll be fine. I've been through worse," he replied, in such a way as to make me think that his pride was doing a lot of work to cover his genuine feelings, but I didn't have the energy to try and peel away the layers of his soul to get to the truth underneath. It wouldn't have helped anything anyway. Buck was a strong man, a warrior, and there was nothing that would keep him away from this final battle. It was part of the reason why I loved him, even if it was maddening.

"Thank you for last night. I couldn't cope with being alone," I said, a little embarrassed because it was the first time we had been affectionate with each other. I'd enjoyed it though and liked the fact that he hadn't taken me coming to his bed as an invitation for sex.

"It's okay. I think we both needed it, in a way. I've lived my life in a certain way for a long time Trish, but you're showing me that there are other parts of me, parts that I've neglected for too long."

"I'm glad. Buck...promise me that you'll be safe out there and you won't take any undue risks."

Buck looked at me directly. "I promise," he said. I didn't know if he was lying to me or not. Maybe it didn't matter.

"I just want the three of you to come home. The Hunters have taken so much away from me already...so much away from us."

Buck walked over and placed a hand on my cheek, stopping the flow of my words. "It will all be fine. Jack has a plan. He wouldn't have gone through with this if he didn't think there was a good chance of it succeeding. We're going to be alright," he offered me a slanting smile and the tenor of his voice was soothing. I rose to my feet and wrapped my arms around him in a tight hug. I pressed my head against his shoulder and sniffed back my tears, before kissing him on the cheek. It was a kiss of gratitude that quickly turned into a kiss of passion. My face shifted to the side and his lips caught mine. His breath washed over me and I lost myself in the glory of his embrace. He pulled me tightly towards him, his fingers digging deep into my skin as though he had never learned how to be tender with a woman and only followed his animal lust. I was breathless when we broke apart and staggered back.

"I'll be seeing you," Buck said, and with that he was gone.

*

I was left alone in the clubhouse, vulnerable, and all I could do was wait. I went to the bar and poured myself a drink, and then another, settling on a chair as I looked out at the empty road outside. My throat ran dry as I thought of the battle that must have been raging elsewhere, all the carnage and the mayhem of the war between the two wolf packs. It was so far removed from my current world, which was this quiet place in the middle of nowhere. I smirked to myself and offered myself a wry chuckle as I shot back another drink and wiped the trickling remnants from the corners of my mouth. When I had first come here I had prayed for this to happen. I was free of my captors and could have returned to my life, but now my life was here. Everything before had been false, an illusion. I spared a thought for the people I had left behind, but in truth I hadn't thought too much about them once I'd settled here. I hoped they weren't too sad about losing me. It all seemed so long ago now, that night in the bar where I had sung my heart out. I remembered them now, the three of them looking at me while I sang and how there had been so much pure emotion in their faces. Since I was alone I thought there was no harm in singing again. This time I didn't sing for Mom, I sang for my three wolves.

The sound emerged from my mouth like flowing honey. It was sweet and clear and filled up every corner of the bar. My heart trembled and the more I sang the more intense my emotions became. Soon enough I was sweeping my arms wildly as I moved around the bar, and I could feel some sense of the magic that Jack had been talking about. When I sang I felt connected to all the wolves who had come before and all those who would come after me. I was filled with love for my three wolves and felt proud that they had found me and hadn't hesitated in rescuing me from my ordinary life. I dreaded to think what things would have been like had they not found me, how unhappy I would have been and how I would still have been searching for my purpose.

Eventually the song died down and I was surrounded by silence again. I looked around at the empty bar and knew that I could not stay here. Even though I could not fight, my place was with them. I at least had to see them, to know they were okay, rather than spend time in this purgatory and wait to be told the horrible, terrible news. I grabbed a leather jacket and then walked outside. The sun blinded me as it gleamed off the metal motorcycles. I picked the nearest one and climbed over the saddle, revving the engine. It took a few tries before it roared into life and then the air whipped through my hair as I sped along the road. I felt the vibrations of the bike shuddering through me as I accelerated, following the straight road down to the battlefield, not knowing what I would find, only knowing that I wanted to share their fate, and if they were suffering then I was going to suffer with them.

*

The world was deceptively beautiful. On one side of the road was the lush forest that I had tried to escape through, on the other side was a clear field with mountains rising up in the distance, looking as though they might have been illusory. I could have easily lost myself in the beauty of this world. It was easy to forget that a short distance away there was a battle for the fate of the wolves. I focused my gaze on the road ahead and soon enough the town came into view. I saw the rise of squat buildings first, before I heard the gnashing sounds of wolves clashing. Fear gripped my heart as I slowed, and then my jaw dropped as I saw the first signs of battle. All outside the perimeter of the town were dead bodies, a mass of them, with blood-stained fur and limp limbs sprawled across the ground. Nausea rose within me. It was difficult to tell how many of them were Hunters and how many were Howlers, but from the position of them it seemed as though most of them were facing away from the town, indicating that they were Hunters. I swelled with pride as the pack had succeeded in setting a trap for the Hunters, and with evened odds the Howlers stood a better chance of victory.

Movement to my right caught my attention. A wolf limped around a corner, shuffling along as fast as it could, dragging a wounded leg along the ground. It looked bedraggled and it whimpered, but as soon as it sensed me it snarled and adjusted its direction to come towards me. I was just about to drive away from it when another blur streaked behind it and sank its jaws into the wolf's back. The wolf collapsed and yelped in pain. It put up a weak effort to fight, but it could offer no defense against the stronger wolf. Its throat was torn out, and the wolf collapsed to the ground, a dark shadow of blood spreading out below it. The victorious wolf's jaws were stained with crimson and it turned back, running to rejoin the main battle. I strained my ears and could tell that it was close. I could hear the snarling and the gnashing and the maelstrom. I revved the engine again and was about to drive down the street towards the battle, when I saw a loose plank that had been broken off a rundown house. Four nails protruded from one end. It was narrow enough and light enough for me to wield in one hand, and would serve as a weapon if I needed to defend myself.

I rode down the street and turned a corner, following the noise, fear rising within as I wasn't sure what I was going to find. The road opened up to a town square and my jaw dropped again when I saw what was happening. The wolves were locked in a vicious storm of claws and teeth, the fur blurring and streaking together to create one pattern of color, a rainbow of war that spread like a canvas across the town square. Dead bodies littered the ground, and wounded wolves crawled and whimpered, trying to find some kind of mercy or peace in the midst of battle. I searched for any of my three wolves, but I was unable to see them in amongst the crowd. There were howls and growls, and dust rose around them as they were locked in combat. I couldn't see which side was winning and I suddenly realized just how helpless I was.

Then a wolf ran towards me at full speed. It hurtled through from the crowd after it had spotted me. I tried to kick start the bike, but my foot missed and I slammed against the ground. The wolf moved impossibly fast and when I looked up next it was almost upon me. I screamed as I acted out of instinct and swung my weapon back, bringing it crashing around. The wolf lunged towards me with an open jaw and bared teeth, promising death if it met my flesh, but I had timed my attack well. The plank came crashing round and slammed into the side of its head. The nails tore its flesh and I heard the sickening sound of its skin being punctured. The wolf yelped in pain and was shuffled to the side, its body crashing to the ground. Blood trickled down like tracks of tears, and it dripped off the ends of the nails. I braced myself for another attack as it tried to get up. I steadied myself on the bike, knowing that it was a race against time. If the wolf recovered before I did it would attack again, and I didn't know how well I'd be able to defend myself again.

I kicked the bike and almost cried with relief when it started. The tires screamed as they burst forward just as the wolf was getting to its feet. I tilted my body to the side and swung the plank around again, this time hitting the wolf with more force as I had the added momentum caused by the bike's speed. The nails bit into the wolf's skin and ripped the flesh apart, tearing the wolf's flesh. It pulled the wolf along until the nails came free. It yelped and whimpered as it was dragged along the road, and then it lay silent as the nails broke free. I left behind a dead wolf, and adrenaline surged through my body.

But the commotion of the bike had caught the attention of others. They turned and started to chase after me, and none of them had noble intentions in their eyes. A few of them were behind me and I gulped with fear as I realized I had bitten off more than I could chew. I only had one plank after all, and my only hope was to ride away. But then another wolf came running towards me. I was filled with fear at first, before I saw its golden eyes and realized that it was Jack. He ran beside me and stopped, growling at the onrushing wolves. Another two wolves joined us, Matt and Buck. I was delighted to know that they had survived the battle and were by my side. I turned my bike around, understanding what Jack was trying to tell me. I revved the bike again as the pack of wolves chasing us were still coming, then we moved forward. The three wolves kept up the pace beside me as we attacked like spearmen charging forward. I swung the plank and caught a wolf in the jaw, and as I didn't stop I also rammed another wolf in the side with the bike. Jack, Matt, and Buck attacked with wild abandon. They moved as one unit, swiping with such ferocity and vigor that I didn't believe anyone could stand in their way. I was proud to see them fight, and to see them conquer these malevolent Hunters that thought they were so superior. In the chaos of battle my wolves emerged victorious, leaving behind them carnage and bloodshed, and then they found other wolves to fight.

I couldn't believe how many Hunters there were. They streamed out in a swarm and there always seemed to be more to fight, so much so that I worried there would be too many and all this valiant effort would have been for nothing. I did what I could, using the bike to slalom around the wolves and attack them wherever I could, trying to distract them while other Howlers made their moves, but I wasn't as valuable to the effort as the actual wolf pack and I knew our hopes rested on them. There was one moment when I saw Jack get blindsided by an attack. Two wolves poured on him and swiped at him on the ground. I lost sight of his writhing form amidst the hazy bustle of the fight, but I was filled with a protective urge. I rode towards him and slammed my plank down, finding the flank of one of the wolves. It turned around and swiped at me, almost striking me down from the bike, tearing three claw marks through my leather jacket, but it allowed Jack the opportunity to prove his strength and fight back. He managed to escape and slay the two beasts, and then we rode away to find our next targets.

The longer the battle went on, the less afraid I was, since I was confident in the ability of the wolves to protect me. The pace was frenetic and I didn't really have time to think or be afraid because instinct kicked in, and I wondered if that was how wolves lived all the time. It was impossible to tell how well we were doing in the battle as I couldn't distinguish the wolves by their scent, so I had to be careful and only attack wolves who were obviously the enemy, which I usually decided when they confronted me. There came a moment when the tide turned though, and it became clear that most of the Hunters were laid on the ground, dead or dying. They were fighting to the last wolf, their teeth bared, and their bloodied claws swiping out in wild slashes, more out of hope than of accuracy. They were a dying pack now, and the Howlers pressed their advantage until there were only three Hunters left. I recognized one of them as a wolf who had attacked me in the forest, when I had tried to make my escape.

Their lips snarled as they trembled with anger and backed away, pressing their bodies together in the hope that they might boost their defensive capabilities. The hackles rose on the backs of their necks and their paws pressed tightly against the ground. It looked as though their bodies were coiled like springs, ready to unleash power, and I hoped that they would have more sense than try to attack when they were surrounded.

Jack broke away from the pack and approached them. He howled and pointed to the road. Although I couldn't understand him I got the impression that he was offering them a chance to live another day and rethink the path of their life. They weren't smart enough to take it. The three moved in unison and lunged towards Jack. I gasped in horror as they overwhelmed him and grappled him to the ground, but the other Howlers quickly leapt to his aid and before too long there was nothing left but three more dead bodies.

The threat of the Hunters had been ended. The town was the property of the Howlers once again, and my wolves had stayed alive. It was a time to be celebrated, and my blood was still rushing with adrenaline. I was buzzing as the Howlers tilted their heads back and howled with all their might, announcing to the world that they were the strongest pack, and that this territory was theirs and anyone who disputed that should think twice about challenging them. It was also a signal to all the other wolves that had fled this place, a message that it was safe to come home.

Chapter Eighteen

"Why did you offer them a chance to escape?" Buck asked when we were back in the club house. After killing the final few Hunters the pack had turned back into humans and had taken stock of the toll the day had taken. Good wolves had died, and it was time to mourn them, but they had died defending the pack, and that was something to be proud of. Jack had declared that anyone strong enough should stay and help them clean up the town of the dead bodies, and anyone else should return to the clubhouse and rest. I helped clean up the town, and Jack spoke brightly of the plans to come back to live here. I looked around at the rundown houses and the boarded up windows. It was a place that was unloved, but he seemed convinced that it had potential, so I was as well.

But we were all tired by the time we returned to the club house and repopulating the town was something that could wait for later. I was glad to return, for now we could begin the rest of our lives together and there was something beautifully wonderful about that.

Jack smirked in response to Buck's question. "Because it was the right thing to do; there are certain values that we have to hold true to in this pack, values that have been passed down to us for generations," he looked at me when he said this, "but, really, I wanted them to know that we had defeated them, that after all of this it was us who had their lives in our hands. I knew they would never agree to surrender, but I offered them the choice anyway because I could. I'm just glad we don't have to worry about them anymore, and that we can rebuild the pack properly."

"Something I'm looking forward to," I said with a cheeky smile.

"I think there's something else we need to talk about first," Matt said as he turned to me. "Just what the hell were you doing out there? I thought you were going to stay here where it was safe?"

All three men looked at me with their arms crossed over their chests, judging me like schoolteachers who had caught a student doing something naughty. I dipped my head coyly and blushed a little. "I couldn't handle being here by myself, not knowing what was going on. I figured whatever happened we should share the same fate. If we were going to die, we were going to die together, and if we were going to win, then we should win together too."

"I'm glad it was the latter," Jack said.

I was filled with excitement and my eyes gleamed as I ran up to them, tilting my head up to look at them as they were all so much taller than me. I spread my arms out to bring them all in for an embrace.

"So...how is this going to work?" Buck asked.

"Let's not think about the details at the moment. All I know is that right now I want all three of you. We won together, and we should be together now as well, just as a pack should be." I hugged and kissed each of them in turn, chaste and sweet, and then I looked at them expectantly, wondering which of them was going to make the first move.

*

It was Jack of course. He thrust his arm out and wrapped his hand around the back of my neck, pulling me forward abruptly, the movement so swift that the air rushed out of my lungs and I was left breathless with a hard kiss. I was just falling into it when he turned me around and pushed me to Matt, who kissed me as well, and then finally I was in Buck's arms. My mind whirled as I was passed between the three men, loving the thought of being in their arms and feeling the heat from their bodies. I was already burning inside and ready to be theirs, to give myself to the wolf pack. My desire for the three of them blended together and created this miasma of pleasure that surged through my entire body and made my skin glisten with sweat. I trembled and felt my knees turn to water. I was strong and weak all at the same time, and all I wanted was to serve these men. They stepped forward, encasing me in a cocoon of flesh, a tight circle where just the three of them were the only things that mattered to me in the entire world. I reached out and touched their bodies, I let their hands coil around me, slithering like serpents dragging me down into a dark abyss, yet there was nothing terrifying or terrible about this. It was freedom, it was light, it was beautiful.

When the fire of Buck's kiss echoed on my lips, it felt as though I had been intoxicated by a potent cocktail that was a mix of all three of them. The air crackled with vibrant electricity and a fluttering sensation rose through my mind, rippling out like the music from a tender song. Everywhere I turned there was a powerful man, a wolf, ready to claim me. Then I felt pressure on my shoulders and I sank to my knees. They already towered above me, but now they were like giants and I was so small, completely at their mercy, and the air simmered with the heat of their arousal.

I couldn't resist reaching out and touching their bodies. My hands brushed over the swelling arousal that tightened their jeans, and something inside me twitched. A deep ache burned in my molten core and I was filled with a need to have more. I fumbled with their belts, trying to undo all three at once, but I only had two hands so I had to use my teeth to slip away one of the leather straps. It came free with a satisfying sound and I enjoyed the murmurs of the men. Their hands came down and helped me where I needed it, unleashing their erections and my mouth dropped open with shock and desire. They were each beautiful in their own way, thick and long, hard and taut, with rippling veins. Dark hair shadowed the bases and smooth tips gazed at me, begging to be sucked and licked and pleasured. A deep, primal hunger swelled within me and I immediately dared to reach out and touch them. I curled my fingers around the three erections, moving my hands between them to try and give each of them equal attention. I brushed their skin and teased their thighs and watched their throbbing power being displayed before me. I had a wide grin on my face as I looked up at my wolves and then began to pleasure them. I wrapped my lips around Jack's cock and sucked it deep and slow, coating it in my saliva, before I turned my head and did the same to Matt's, and then Buck's. While I sucked one I used my hands to pleasure the others. It was a dance that was as choreographed as a ballet.

Instinct came over me completely as my mind grew hazy and delirious. I was so aware of the sensations coursing through my body that I lost sense of everything else. I was utterly a part of them, a tool for their pleasure, and in turn I received pleasure of my own. They tasted so good. Their heat scorched my mouth and tongue, and it wasn't long before my jaw began to ache, but the pain was sweet and only reminded me that I was doing a good thing; that I was making them feel good and repaying their faith in me. Drool trickled over my sore lips. My hands moved in a blur, stroking tight skin as my groans were muffled when I gagged on their erections. A hand grabbed a fistful of my hair and pulled my head back. I winced in pain as I felt the heat being smeared across my face. My hands fell limply by my sides as I was overwhelmed by all this passion, but then I regained my senses somewhat and let them rise again, not wanting to let go of them or for any of them to miss out on any pleasure. I was determined to pleasure them all and the need was so vibrant inside me that I had to get closer to them. I brought them together, bringing my hands closer to my mouth. Groggy, my vision was blurred, but my instincts were sharp and I knew exactly what I had to do. I opened my mouth wide as I pressed their erections together and managed to fit all three tips in my mouth at once. Foamy saliva drooled out of me and splashed on the floor. I groaned loudly, and their terse moans were music to my ears, a devilish chorus that inspired the darkest most tempting parts of me.

Then a hand dragged me away. More than one hand. All three of them were touching me and I was overwhelmed by the sensation of being manhandled like this. I was flung to the bed and landed with a crash. I was soon pulled away, barely given a chance to regain my composure. My head hung back and my hair fell down like a waterfall. I felt my legs being pulled apart as my clothes were ripped away, torn to shreds as the wild animals treated me like their prey, displaying their masculine strength, a strength that could not have been denied even if I had been reluctant to fulfill their desires. My mouth hung open and long, guttural moans trembled out of me, as my flushed skin prickled with desire. There was a deep ache in my body, an ache that would not be calmed unless they did something about it.

I watched with bleary eyes as Matt sank to his knees before me. Buck and Jack stood either side of me, their pleasure still rampant in their bodies. They fondled my breasts and I continued sucking their erections as Matt's hand brushed my burning inner thighs. My body surrendered and I melted as I felt his breath against my femininity. Then a darting tongue started dancing with my body. The heat and the wetness spread and my thighs became slick. His long hair splayed out across my legs as he buried himself in me and pleasure rippled all over my body in a fervent wave.

The world swirled around me in a blur and I rocked violently as the cascading orgasm rippled and burst through like a tidal wave, far more quickly and more passionately than I had ever experienced before. The dam had broken and there was still more, I could feel it growing inside me. The thought of bracing myself against it all was daunting and I didn't know if I could handle it, but if I was going to be broken then I would welcome it gladly as long as it was by these three men. My lips were stolen in a kiss as hands roamed around my body, exploring my supple flesh and finding all the sweet parts. All the while Matt continued pleasuring me. There were so many sensations my mind could barely keep up and I had no idea what was happening, only that quaking pleasure flooded out of me in delicious waves.

Eventually Matt rose to kiss me and I tasted my own sweetness on his lips. He hooked his arm around my body and before I knew it he was inside me. I leaned back, my body arching, my legs hooked around him. His head was buried in the crook of my neck as his lean, slender body crashed into me with a desire that had been present from the first time we met. I clutched his back and dragged my nails down his skin as I felt him tremble and tense, knowing that he was ready to give me everything. Moans crashed against me and I didn't care that it was so soon, he had made me melt with his tongue and now I wanted everything he had to give me. I coaxed him with seductive whispers and felt his body shudder as the warmth shot into me like shards shooting away from a broken planet.

I barely had time to kiss him before I was torn away and pushed onto my knees, my head forced down and a cock shoved in my mouth. I looked up and saw Jack standing above me, and then felt two hands around my waist, holding me tightly, squeezing me and then I felt something else, something big, something that made me groan. Buck showed no mercy as he plunged himself inside me and picked up from where Matt had left off, grabbing a fistful of my hair as he fucked me roughly, slamming into me with the force of an earthquake. Tears streamed down my cheeks as the exquisite agony surged through me and I was carried by this blurring of pain and pleasure to paradise once again, my consciousness lifting through my body.

All the while I was doing my best to pleasure Jack, to keep sucking even though my jaw felt as though it was going to drop off. Buck crashed into me. I could feel the bruises swelling over my skin where he held me so tightly, where he let his passion flow free and gave me everything he had. The snarling grunts of passion were the same sounds he had made in battle. He was a warrior, a strong, powerful man who only ever gave something his full energy. My body cracked under the weight of his intensity and I felt like everything was taken for me as he gave me his orgasm. It was as hot as a volcano and erupted violently. When he was done he pushed me forward. Jack fell back, catching my trembling body in his arms. I whimpered and couldn't even form a thought let alone a sentence. My hair was matted to my skin and I felt as though I had been shattered, and Jack was picking up the pieces and putting me back together again. I crawled onto him and our bodies came together. I wrapped my arms around his neck and nestled into him as he slipped into me and I rode him. Mercifully he went gently, tenderly, and gave me all the love that he had. We kissed and my body started to move with his rhythm. Pleasure ran around my body again, this time with the force of a supernova, and when I came I kissed him deeply, hoping that he could sense the depth of my feelings, hoping that he welcomed everything that I could give him.

He held me still for a long time after he came, as though the moment would last forever. Then, he let me slip away. Buck and Matt were already laid on the bed, drained, their sweat soaked bodies glistening, their powerful chests heaving. I sank in between them, still surrounded by all this burning, vibrant flesh that was such a pleasure for me. I reached out with my shaking hands to caress them and I closed my eyes, breathing in all the scents and feeling the heat simmering inside me. My body had been given more than it could handle and I felt as though I had been broken, but it was a welcome sensation and even then I knew that I wanted it again. I was complete with these three men in a way that I could never have been with just one of them. They were my wolves, my lovers, and I couldn't imagine life without them.

They each reached out and placed a hand upon my quaking body. I closed my eyes and smiled, whispering my love for them. It was finally over. I was finally where I belonged; with my wolves.

Epilogue

The sun shone brightly above me as I sat on the porch, sipping my lemonade. The drink was refreshing and I sighed happily as I rested my hand against my swollen belly. The town had changed over the past few years and now it was almost impossible to believe it had been ramshackle and abandoned. The Howlers had their home back again, and they had made it their own, or our own I should say. The streets were filled with happy people and at night wolves were free to roam around without fear of being hunted or attacked. Nobody here had to hide who they were, and it was the most wonderful place in the world to live. I was happier than I had ever been before and I couldn't believe that I had ever thought my destiny lay away from the wolves. I thought back to my first moment when I had been taken away by my lovers, how afraid I had been, and it made me smile. It was all a part of the journey.

"Mom, can we go and play?!" Jake asked, bursting out of the house with Tanya in tow. Jake was the eldest. Tanya was followed by the crawling Catherine, who was eager to follow her elder siblings despite the fact that she could barely walk yet. The three of them had different fathers and yet I could see the qualities of Jack, Matt, and Buck in each of them. If anyone had told me that I would have ended up with three partners I would have laughed them away because it seemed far too confusing, but somehow we made it work. We all supported each other and helped out with the kids, and over the years we had found a natural rhythm. Now, I couldn't imagine any other way of living life.

"Sure thing, but don't stay out for too long, and make sure you have plenty to drink, it's a warm day," I said. Jake and Tanya threw their fists in the air and yelped with delight as they scampered away, not heeding my warning at all. Catherine crawled over the porch intending to follow her siblings, but I picked her up and set her on my lap. She squirmed and writhed in my arms, twisting and pointing at her brother and sister, but she soon settled when I gave her a cuddle. They were enough of a handful now, they would be even worse when they could change into wolves. Hopefully, by that point I'd be ready for the challenge.

A shadow loomed over the porch as Buck approached. I looked up and smiled. He leaned down to kiss me on the cheek. He wore his customary denim vest and had a bag slung over his shoulder.

"Is this finally it then?" I asked.

"I figure I've been threatening to do it for long enough, I might as well actually go through with it," he said.

"Good, I'm glad. I feel as though I've been nagging you about it forever," I smiled.

"Well, I've never been this sure that Jack and Matt can handle things around here by themselves."

"And what about me?"

"You've had your hands full," Buck said, reaching out and playing with Catherine's hair. She giggled as his hand stroked her soft cheek, and she leaned into him. "I'm going to miss her. I'm going to miss all of them." The slanting smile disappeared from his face and he looked pensive. I reached up with my free hand and clutched his, squeezing it gently.

"It's okay, you'll be back soon enough, and you'll have a good story to tell," I said.

"I hope so," Buck said. "I'm not sure he'll be happy to see me though."

"He's your father, of course he will be, and even if he's not, you'll feel better for making the attempt."

"I know, it's just going to be difficult at first, but I've been putting it off for long enough," Buck said with a long sigh. "No, it'll be okay. It'll be good to tell him that things have gotten better and that the Hunters aren't a problem anymore. I'm looking forward to telling him that we've rebuilt this place and that we're raising a strong generation of new wolves."

"Do you think he'll come back?"

"Probably not. He has his life and his career, but maybe one day he'll visit. I'm sure he'll want to see his grandchildren."

"I hope so. It'll be good to meet him."

"I'll be seeing you Trish, and once I'm back maybe I'll have someone new to meet," he said, patting my stomach. I laughed as he kissed me goodbye. It was going to be a strain to live without Buck for a little while, but it was important for him to see his father. I hoped that Buck's dad would come back and live with us because it was important for the community to grow. We had done well at getting word out to other wolves, and there were already other women who had helped me bring forth a new generation. As I watched the children run through the streets of the city I thought about the future and felt blessed that I could watch a new world grow before my eyes. I was certain that mom and dad would be looking down on me with pride. Before I had encountered the wolves I had been struggling to find the place in the world where I belonged, but with them I had found my purpose, I had found my happiness.

I picked up Catherine and walked down the porch after I finished my lemonade. "Come on, let's go and see your fathers," I said, with a smile on my face and tranquility in my heart. It had been a long journey getting to this point, but it had all been worth it.

*****

Don't miss out!

Visit the website below and you can sign up to receive emails whenever Lilly Wilder publishes a new book. There's no charge and no obligation.

https://books2read.com/r/B-A-KAQD-WCVDC

Connecting independent readers to independent writers.

Also by Lilly Wilder